"Your aunt insisted I stay at your home," Phoebe said, "but I can already see that I'll be inconveniencing you. Can you tell me where the nearest boardinghouse is?"

Phoebe *was* inconveniencing them…what could Chance say to that, except that it was the truth?

"I hear you've met my daughter," he said instead.

"I have," she agreed with a smile that didn't quite meet her eyes. "And while I think she's lovely, I don't believe I made quite the same impression on her."

Chance smothered a chuckle as he imagined this well-spoken city girl bumping heads with his straight-talking tomboy daughter. That would have been a sight to see.

Phoebe lifted an eyebrow. Her hazel eyes were glistening, as if she were trying to hold back tears. He wondered if she was, and if he was the cause of it.

Probably. And that stung.

He didn't like that one bit.

Books by Deb Kastner

Love Inspired

A Holiday Prayer
Daddy's Home
Black Hills Bride
The Forgiving Heart
A Daddy at Heart
A Perfect Match
The Christmas Groom
Hart's Harbor
Undercover Blessings
The Heart of a Man
A Wedding in Wyoming
His Texas Bride
The Marine's Baby
A Colorado Match
Phoebe's Groom

*Email Order Brides

DEB KASTNER

Deb Kastner lives and writes in colorful Colorado with the Front Range of the Rocky Mountains for inspiration. She loves writing for the Love Inspired line, where she can write about her two favorite things—faith and love. Her characters range from upbeat and humorous to (her favorite) dark and broody heroes. Her plots fall anywhere in between, from a playful romp to the deeply emotional. Deb's books have been twice nominated for the *RT Book Reviews* Reviewer's Award for Best Book of the Year for Love Inspired. Deb and her husband share their home with their two youngest daughters. Deb is thrilled about the newest member of the family—her first granddaughter, Isabella. What fun to be a granny! Deb loves to hear from her readers. You can contact her by email at DEBWRTR@aol.com, or on her MySpace or Facebook pages.

Phoebe's Groom

Deb Kastner

Love Inspired

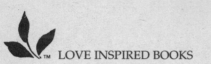

™ LOVE INSPIRED BOOKS

ISBN-13: 978-0-373-81560-9

PHOEBE'S GROOM

I waited patiently for the Lord;
He turned to me and heard my cry.
He lifted me out of the slimy pit,
Out of the mud and mire;
He set my feet on a rock
And gave me a firm place to stand.
He put a new song in my mouth,
A hymn of praise to our God.
Many will see and fear
And put their trust in the Lord God.
—*Psalm* 40:1–3

For those who have loved and lost—
may God give you peace and comfort

Prologue

STATUS UPDATE: PHOEBE YATES: I'm tired. I absolutely love what I'm doing, and I'm grateful to God for all the blessings He's given me, but sometimes I long for a less demanding lifestyle

JOSPEHINE HAWKINS MURPHY: I imagine you are, dear. Being so accomplished can be hard on anyone, even a chef.

PHOEBE YATES: LOL. I don't view myself as especially gifted.

JOSEPHINE HAWKINS MURPHY: Trust me, dear, you're as talented as they come.

PHOEBE YATES: Sigh. I think I need a vacation.

JOSEPHINE HAWKINS MURPHY: A break from baking?

PHOEBE YATES: Oh, goodness, no. Once a pastry chef, always a pastry chef. Baking is what I do for fun, to relax. It's just the frenzied schedule that's driving me crazy.

JOSEPHINE HAWKINS MURPHY: In that case, dear, I think I may be able to help.

Chapter One

STATUS UPDATE: PHOEBE YATES: Day 1 of my adventure into country living. First observation: Serendipity, Texas, is a small town. A *VERY* small town.

JOSEPHINE HAWKINS MURPHY: Indeed it is, dear. Indeed it is.

Maybe this was a bad idea, Phoebe Yates thought to herself as she pulled her luxury rental car in front of the rickety, clapboard-sided diner called Cup O' Jo.

Probably this was a mistake.

She supposed she could turn around right now, head back to the airport in San Antonio and fly back to her hometown of New York City. No one yet knew she was here in Serendipity, Texas. She could just cry off and make up an excuse for why she hadn't been able to make it.

But she'd given her word to Josephine Hawkins Murphy, and since Phoebe was a Christian, her word meant everything. Besides, she was here because she'd wanted a break from her high-profile, culinary lifestyle. This six-week sabbatical from her close-to-insane schedule before she was due to start as head pastry chef at a new, upscale restaurant in Times Square was just what she needed. She just hadn't realized Serendipity was going to be quite this small.

One main street cut through the entire town, with only two stop signs located on opposite ends. Besides the café, there was a gas station, a hardware store, Sam's Grocery, a barber shop with a candy cane–striped pole on the sign and a little white chapel with red doors and a steeple.

This town was tiny.

To her credit, Jo had warned her as much from the start, but Phoebe really didn't have anything to compare it with, having lived in a big city all her life.

Exiting the car, she smoothed down her pure cotton, sky-blue dress, grimaced and sighed. Thanks to the long drive, the material was full of wrinkles. Oh, well. From the look of things, she was probably overdressed, even for a job interview, which was, more or less, what she was here for.

Yet another challenge with the town of Serendipity—it didn't even have a hotel. Otherwise, she would have checked in first and freshened up before stopping by the café.

Jo had assured her she'd have a place to stay, though the details were vague. Not for the first time, Phoebe felt a wave of uneasiness steal over her. This was way, *way* out of her comfort zone.

She'd prayed about this, she reminded herself firmly. Onward and forward. She wasn't a coward.

The moment she stepped into the diner, she was immediately and joyfully accosted by an ample, smiling elderly woman whom Phoebe immediately recognized as Jo from her online profile photograph. Her bouncing red curls gave her away in an instant. She was wearing an equally bright red T-shirt that boasted the phrase "I'm right, you're wrong, any questions?"

Phoebe only had a moment for a quick assessment of the café itself, but it was clear that while the outside of the diner was rustic, the inside had clearly been remodeled with a contemporary coffee-shop feel.

Even with Jo's warm welcome, Phoebe was aware she'd been put on the spot. It felt as if everyone in the room had frozen in place, some with forks halfway to their mouths, some staring over the rims of the computer monitors that outlined the back wall.

They were all watching her, as if waiting for…

Something.

And when conversation once again resumed, it was like listening to the drone of a hive of bees. She had no doubt they were speaking about her. The thought didn't make her as uncomfortable as it could have.

She was used to people talking about her. She couldn't be successful in her career for long without positive publicity, not to mention criticism. She wondered which was relevant now. Maybe both.

Exclaiming in delight, Jo wrapped her arms around Phoebe, hugging her as if they'd known each other for a lifetime and not only just met. Phoebe didn't know what to do with that. She wasn't used to such adamant affection, especially publically so, and she found herself intensely uncomfortable with the inexplicable familiarity Jo showed her.

They hadn't even been formally introduced, though they'd corresponded online, which had resulted in her being here in the first place. Phoebe was Jo's deceased husband's cousin several times removed. At least that's what Jo had said when she'd made her friend request.

It was an unusual experience for her to feel welcomed—*really* welcomed—anywhere, especially with the ease, grace, and naturally friendly demeanor Jo obviously possessed.

"Everyone," Jo announced in a voice that pierced right through the buzz of conversation in the room, "this here is Phoebe Yates, and she's our new pastry chef."

Happily, thought Phoebe, Jo didn't mention her high-profile status. She had the feeling it was going to be tough enough to make friends in this close-knit community without adding that fact into the mix. Some patrons were openly staring at her, while others merely smiled politely and turned back to their meals, drinks or computer screens.

Once again, she felt that the rising hum of voices had something to do with her arrival in town, but she brushed any awkwardness aside. From what she'd seen thus far, she doubted Serendipity had many strangers passing through, so it made sense that she'd be a novelty for them. Besides, she'd been in the spotlight before, and most of the smiles were curious and friendly.

What did she have to worry about?

She was, she decided firmly, going to like it here. Cup O' Jo Café was out in the middle of nowhere, which was just what she needed. And if the glass-cased pastry shelves at the front counter were anything to go by, they needed her as well. Currently they housed a number of old knickknacks, rather than anything edible. That was something Phoebe definitely could fix for them.

"This way, dear," Jo said, indicating the hunter-green swinging doors which led to the kitchen. "Let me show you where you will be working, and then we'll get you settled in so you can rest up after all that traveling. I imagine you must be exhausted."

Phoebe smiled. This really was an adventure, in

the best sense of the word. "I'm good. And I'd love to check out the kitchen."

Her excitement died the moment she walked through the double doors and met the cool, black-eyed gaze of the man at the grill. He held a spatula in one hand almost like a weapon, and his frown and the furrowing of his brow deepened with every step Phoebe took in his direction.

He was tall and broad-shouldered and his jet-black hair spilled over his forehead and curled at his neck. His face was chiseled and sharply planed, giving him a rugged look. He wore a denim shirt, faded blue jeans, scuffed black cowboy boots that looked like they'd seen better days and a stained white apron tied around a lean waist.

He had loosely tied a black bandana around his neck, giving him the appearance of an old-time bank robber, and Phoebe thought it might somehow match his personality, or what she could tell of it. He might be extremely attractive were it not for the scowl on his face, but his shadowy frown ruined everything.

"Chance, dear," Jo said, bursting into the kitchen just behind Phoebe. "Welcome our new pastry chef, Phoebe Yates. Phoebe, this is my nephew, Chance Hawkins. He does all of the cooking here. I'd be lost without him."

His scowl deepened, if that were possible, and his black eyes sparked with displeasure. Phoebe recognized the man's type immediately. After all, she'd worked with enough of them over the years.

The angry chef.

A man who'd never learned to share his toys, much less his kitchen.

And it was apparent, from the shocked, astounded expression he flashed Jo that she'd neglected to mention the fact that Phoebe would be here at all.

At least his features evened out when he looked at his aunt. Definitely not friendly, but not as openly hostile as that first, undefined moment when he had been caught off guard. As Phoebe had first suspected, he was a handsome man, in a rugged sort of way.

"Pastry chef?" Chance queried, his voice low and raspy. "No offense, ma'am," he continued, flashing his dark gaze briefly to Phoebe before returning to Jo, "but I wasn't told about this, and it isn't a good idea."

No offense? Chance Hawkins had offense written all over him with a figurative pen.

What had she gotten herself into? She'd come here to get away from drama, not step right into the middle of it.

Jo simply chuckled, not at all offended by Chance's gruff nature and harsh voice. "In case you didn't notice, we have knickknacks on the shelves of the pastry rack. Me, I'd rather have dessert."

"But Aunt Jo, you know I don't—" He paused,

brushing his hands down the front of his apron and adjusting the bandana at his neck, which Phoebe thought might be a nervous gesture. "I can't."

Jo stepped forward, directly in front of Chance, and ran a soothing, affectionate hand over the stubble on his cheek, as if he were a small boy.

"You can," she said softly, in a voice that made Phoebe's throat tighten with an unnamed emotion. "You need to do this. You know you do. Besides, our customers miss having pastries around here."

Phoebe averted her gaze, feeling as if she were intruding on a private family moment.

She surveyed the small but well-stocked kitchen, distracting herself by wondering how she and Chance would be able to share the space. Even if he agreed to Jo's proposal, which at the moment didn't seem likely, there wasn't much counter space, and there was only one small oven. Even if they were trying to avoid it, the two of them would be constantly walking into each other.

She turned her attention back to Chance and Jo as the room became silent. Chance was staring at her, an unreadable look in his midnight-black eyes. His lips tightened as he surveyed her, apparently weighing his options.

Phoebe pulled her shoulders straight and stood an inch taller, and then she smiled at Chance. She might feel a little intimidated by this mixed welcome, but she wasn't about to show it. He could think what he wanted. She was not afraid of all his bluster.

"I don't have a choice in this, do I, Jo?" he asked, his voice still raspy. Phoebe wondered if the low, abrasive tone was how he always talked, or whether it had something to do with him being annoyed at her presence.

"I can't imagine why you thought for a moment that you did," Jo replied with a chuckle.

The corner of his mouth twitched upward as he nodded at Jo, but his gaze was serious when it returned to Phoebe.

"We need to talk, you and I," he told her, his expression guarded.

It sounded like he was telling her, not asking her, and Phoebe bristled. She could only imagine all the things he wanted to say to her. She herself could think of at least a dozen reasons why this scenario wasn't going to work, and she was certain he had even more to add. She only wished she might have known what she was getting into before she'd traveled all the way out west.

Jo obviously believed she was doing the right thing for her nephew, and no doubt she had her reasons for not telling him that Phoebe was coming, but Chance wasn't the only one who had been taken off guard.

Jo hadn't informed Phoebe that the kitchen staff, such as it was, would be blatantly and openly averse to her being here.

This wasn't her fight. She'd come out here for some peace and quiet, not to be placed in the middle of a family squabble. She was uncomfortable just thinking about it.

"I'm sure there are many details that you two will want to hash out about how this kitchen will be run," Jo said, linking her arm through Phoebe's. "But that will have to wait, Chance, dear. Phoebe has only just arrived in town and I'm sure she'll want to get a good night's sleep before tackling any—specifics."

Chance bit his bottom lip as if straining not to speak, but after a moment he gave a clipped nod.

Phoebe frowned. A "good night's sleep" would do little to address the problems she sensed were unspoken and unresolved, but she supposed sleeping on it wouldn't hurt. She *was* fatigued from the long flight and the tedious drive, and it wasn't like she had anywhere else to go—at least not tonight.

"See you later, dear," Jo told Chance as she whisked Phoebe out of the kitchen and dining area, giving swift, pleasant-voiced instructions to a teenage girl, Shelley, who sported a swinging bleach-blond ponytail and was carrying a pot of steaming coffee in each hand.

It might be a small café in a small town, but the place was lively with customers, and Phoebe noted that it appeared to be short of help, if Shelley was the only one left to cover waiting tables while Jo was gone. She had the distinct impression that Chance, like most cooks, wouldn't leave his kitchen to wait on guests or bus tables, even though Cup O' Jo was a family-owned restaurant and he might well have at least part ownership of it.

But in her experience, chefs were royalty, and the kitchens were their castles. And unlike Jo, Chance didn't strike Phoebe as being the outgoing type. He'd probably let poor Shelley run herself ragged before offering to help.

If he offered at all.

She stopped herself mid-thought when she realized she was being completely uncharitable. She was making all kinds of unfair assumptions about Chance without really getting to know him, she chided herself. She knew better than to take someone's character upon a first meeting. It was unlike her to be so judgmental, and she promised herself she would do better, even as she asked God for forgiveness.

"If you'll follow me, Old Bessie is around back," Jo said, breaking into her thoughts.

"Bessie?" Phoebe repeated, confused. She hadn't recalled Jo mentioning a Bessie in their correspondence.

Jo chuckled. "My truck. My husband, Paul, God rest his soul, named her." She sighed deeply, and her pale green eyes took on a hazy, faraway look. "I know it sounds silly, but continuing to call the truck by Paul's pet name makes me feel close to him."

"It's not silly," Phoebe assured her. "And I'm so sorry for your loss."

"Oh, my dear, don't be. Paul has been gone these ten years now, and we had a long and happy marriage together while he was here on earth. Now he's awaitin' me in glory. I'll see him again soon enough."

Phoebe smiled and patted Jo on the shoulder. She already felt closer to this woman than to any of the people back home, even her friends. It was nice to hear her talk so comfortably about her Christian faith, as if she were chatting about the weather. She especially envied the way Jo talked about Paul. Phoebe wasn't sure there was such a thing as a long and happy marriage, but if there was, it couldn't happen to a nicer person than Jo.

"I'll be around in a moment, dear, and then you can follow me home."

"Home? *Your* home? Oh, my. That's not necessary. I know there isn't a hotel nearby, but surely there's a bed-and-breakfast where I can stay, or an apartment where I can get a short-term lease."

"Don't be silly," Jo chided. "There's no reason for you to be paying rent when I have an extra bedroom all set up and ready for you."

"I don't want to be a burden," Phoebe protested.

"Nonsense," Jo replied. "Now, I won't hear another word about it. Get yourself behind the wheel of that fancy car there and follow me to your new home."

Home. Phoebe's own parents had moved to Florida, and she'd been alone for years. She wasn't sure she remembered the meaning of the word *home,* much less in the context of a small town like Serendipity and a family which included Jo Murphy and Chance Hawkins, but she had the feeling she was about to find out.

Chapter Two

STATUS UPDATE: PHOEBE YATES: Things aren't going quite as I expected. The truth is, I guess I didn't really know what I expected. Not this. It may be a very short adventure, after all.

JOSEPHINE HAWKINS MURPHY: Now don't you give up on us yet, dear. Things will work out. You'll see.

Chance settled his worn buckskin cowboy hat on his head and pulled it low over his eyes, and then shrugged into a trench coat of the same color. Being late spring in west Texas, the air still had a definite nip to it, and the wind was always blowing; but he was walking home anyway.

He always walked.

He closed his eyes against the sharp, stabbing

wave of pain that descended on him every time he thought of driving.

Of Lindsay.

He locked the back door of the café behind him, though there was little need for that in Serendipity, where many people didn't so much as take the keys from the ignitions of their cars, much less lock the doors.

Adjusting the bandana around his neck to a more comfortable position, he traced the scar that ran from the corner of his jaw to his collarbone. The physical scar was easily hidden by the cloth. It was what was inside that couldn't be stitched up, that would probably never heal.

Not even after four long, painful years. At this point he doubted if such wounds could ever truly mend. He wasn't even sure he wanted them to, since those tender jabs of pain were all the feelings he had left.

Besides that, he was empty. Void. Hardly what a man could even call human, so distant had he become from the life he'd once known.

And yet life continued, such as it was. Get up every morning. Go to work. Come home again, do chores. Try to sleep, though rest never came easily to him and nightmares plagued him.

He was empty inside, just going through the motions. He wasn't sure he'd even do that were it not for his thirteen-year-old daughter, Lucy, and the fact that Aunt Jo depended on him to keep the café running.

He wasn't going to let Aunt Jo down, and he certainly wasn't going to fail Lucy. For her, he at least had to try, even if he failed on a daily basis. That little girl was the sunshine in his otherwise dark life.

Okay, so maybe Lucy was not *quite* so little anymore, though he was loath to admit it, even to himself. Chance's heart twisted at the thought.

Lucy was moving into her teen years with an alacrity that frightened him. It was bad enough that she'd had to grow up so fast after her mother had died. He hadn't been able to help her much then, and he knew he'd be less than useless when it came to female hormones and mood swings.

Lately, that was all he seemed to be getting from her. She was driving him crazy. He'd never been real good at trying to figure out the female mind, and he'd quickly discovered that reading a *teenage* female mind was so far beyond him it wasn't even funny.

He was useless. But that didn't stop his throat from tightening when he reached the house and Lucy bounded down the front steps to meet him. She had the light brown hair and emerald-green eyes of her mother, and his heart tugged yet again. His little tomboy still wore denim overalls most of the time, and today was no exception.

"What's up?" he said by way of greeting. He held his arms out to her and she gave him a quick, awkward hug. He held her, even when she tried to pull back. Something was obviously bothering her.

"You know," he continued when she didn't immediately speak, "you used to meet me by the door all the time when you were a little rug rat."

She brushed him away with a huff, where he'd expected a giggle, since he'd been teasing her. She was frowning and scowling and he only now noticed her eyes were puffy, as if she'd been crying.

"What's wrong, sweetheart?" he asked, wrapping his arm around her thin shoulders, troubled that it had taken him so long to realize Lucy was upset.

"It's her," Lucy said, her voice muffled by the sleeve of his shirt.

"Who, honey?" he asked, confused by her vague reply. "Did something happen to one of your friends at school?"

"Auntie Jo said she was going to live with us for a while and stay in the extra bedroom. Of our house! She can't do that, Daddy. I don't want her here."

Chance's stomach knotted with suspicion as he navigated his way through his daughter's harsh, emotional words. She had called him *Daddy*. She never called him that unless she was really upset.

Lucy still hadn't told him who *she* was, but he already knew.

"Is her name Ms. Yates?" he asked, trying not to grind his teeth.

"I don't know." Lucy shrugged, both answering

his question and pulling away from his fatherly embrace. "Auntie Jo just called her Phoebe."

"Phoebe," he repeated softly, though alarms with the intensity of fire trucks were blaring in his head.

Aunt Jo wouldn't do that, not without talking to him first. She couldn't. It was bad enough that it appeared he'd have to share his kitchen at work with the stranger. He was none too happy about that.

But his house? No way.

This was the place where he and Lindsay had shared their lives together, and it was the only home Lucy had ever known. Hadn't Aunt Jo thought about how this would affect him and Lucy? It wasn't like her to be insensitive, especially considering she'd only moved in with them after Lindsay's death. It was *his* house. He'd just have to talk to her—get her to see reason.

"Tell you what," he said, giving Lucy an affectionate pat on the shoulder. "You go feed the horses for me, and I'll have a talk with Auntie Jo. I'm sure there's been some kind of mistake."

He *hoped* Lucy had misread the situation, but the disgruntled look she flashed him didn't bode well.

"I heard what I heard," she informed him, her voice higher and thinner than usual. "For your information, I'm not making this up."

"Of course you're not, honey," he assured her. "I'm sorry if I made it sound like you were. What I meant was, maybe I can talk your great-aunt out of it."

Lucy frowned and tilted her head. "Yeah. Well, good luck with that."

She whirled around and stalked toward the barn, her brown braid swinging behind her like the tail of a raccoon. Chance knew he shouldn't have let her get away with sassing him the way she had, but he didn't know what he could say that would fix the problem. The most important thing to him right now was not to alienate her by making her apologize. They needed to be able to put up a united front, especially since it appeared Aunt Jo was going to be on the other side of the battle.

Watching Lucy walk away, he decided to let it go. The poor girl was upset, after all, and rightly so.

He shook his head in bemusement. One second she was running into his arms for comfort, and the next she was talking back to him.

He didn't know what to do with her. Lindsay would have known, but she wasn't here.

And he didn't have time to wallow in his grief. There was a stranger in his house, probably busy unpacking her things while he lingered outside with his thoughts. There was no time to waste.

Stepping into the foyer, he first shed his trench coat, hanging it, along with his hat, on a coat rack near the front door. His muscles tensed as he began searching the house room by room. If she was here, and he had no doubt she was, she'd probably be in the spare bedroom, but he couldn't help but inspect the rest of the house first, his hackles raised like a cougar stalking its prey.

His mind circled his options. If Phoebe had already unpacked, it wouldn't be easy to get her to leave, especially if Aunt Jo had already asked her to stay. He could go around Aunt Jo and order her to leave anyway, but he wasn't sure it would be worth it in the long run to butt heads with the older woman.

What he wanted was peace and quiet in his own household, but that didn't look like it was going to happen, at least not easily. Maybe he could just take Phoebe aside and ask her *politely* to find other lodgings.

Except there weren't any, not in Serendipity. Up until this moment, he hadn't really considered the position Phoebe was in—if she didn't stay at the house, where would she go? There wasn't a single hotel or inn for miles, for the simple reason that Serendipity rarely had visitors, and when they came, they were usually family. The closest thing to family Phoebe had here was some distant relationship with Aunt Jo.

But that wasn't really his problem, was it?

None of this was his idea. Aunt Jo hadn't said a word to him, which was problematic—and annoying. But if Lucy was upset by Phoebe's presence, then his concern immediately escalated from four-alarm to five-alarm. The truth was, this whole matter troubled him more than he cared to admit on any number of levels—an attractive woman in his age range staying at his house. He could just hear the gossips humming.

But at the end of the day, the fierce compulsion to protect his daughter trumped anything else he might be feeling. And that was what he intended to act on.

The door to the spare bedroom was open. There was no sign of Aunt Jo, but Phoebe sat straight-backed on the far corner of the bed, her hands folded serenely in her lap as she stared out the window. Long, straight chestnut-colored hair cascaded over her shoulders. Her suitcase lay at her feet, apparently unopened.

She stiffened when Chance rapped his knuckles against the door frame, though she did not immediately turn to see who was standing at the door.

"I've been waiting for you," she said without so much as a glance in his direction. Presumably, she thought it was Aunt Jo at the door.

"Were you, now?" he asked, expecting to catch her off guard. When she turned to him, he found that her gaze was solemn but not the least bit surprised. She had hazel eyes—an entire palette of browns, greens and blues all mixed together in the most attractive way. That he even *noticed* her eye color alarmed him more than whatever small fright he had hoped to have given her.

Yet one more reason for her *not* to stay in this house, under any conditions.

"Yes," she replied calmly. "Your Aunt Jo insisted

I stay here, but I can already see that I'll be inconveniencing you, and that's the last thing I'd want. Where is the nearest boardinghouse? I'd ask Jo, but she already has her mind set on my staying here, and I'm sure you no doubt realize more than anyone how formidable she can be when she wants something."

Chance snorted. "You've got that right."

Two understatements in a row—Aunt Jo was more than formidable, and as for Phoebe *inconveniencing* them…what could he say to her, except that it was the truth?

"I hear you've met Lucy," he said instead.

"I have," she agreed with a smile that didn't quite meet her eyes. In fact, he thought maybe Lucy had hurt her feelings. He hadn't anticipated that. Phoebe hadn't so much as flinched at his earlier rudeness.

"While I think she's a lovely girl," Phoebe continued wryly, "I don't believe I made quite the same impression on her."

Chance smothered a chuckle as he imagined this well-spoken city girl bumping heads with his straight-talking tomboy daughter. Was it any wonder someone's feelings had been hurt? Although in this case it appeared emotions were raw on both sides.

Phoebe lifted an eyebrow. Her hazel eyes were glistening, as if she was trying to hold back tears. He wondered if she was, and if he—or his daughter—was the cause of it.

Probably.

"So?" she prompted.

Was there a question? He'd forgotten, so he just shrugged and shook his head.

"No, you don't know of any boardinghouses where I can stay, or no, you aren't going to help me?"

Maybe he'd misread her expression. She didn't *sound* like she was about to cry.

Before he could answer, he heard the back door slam. Both of them jumped, startled, like children being caught where they weren't supposed to be.

Lucy. Chance groaned inwardly. Too soon. He hadn't had the opportunity to work things out yet. If she came blustering in here it was just going to make things worse.

"I've got everything I need from the market," came a singsong voice from the kitchen.

Worse than Lucy. Aunt Jo. The small, negligible window of opportunity to send Phoebe off on her merry way without any sort of confrontation with his family had just closed with a resounding bang.

Phoebe apparently thought the same thing.

"So much for that idea," she muttered under her breath, but loud enough for Chance to hear her.

"We'll talk," he promised her; although once Aunt Jo had Phoebe settled in, there was little he'd be able to say to change the situation, and he knew it.

Unfortunately, at the moment, he had a bigger problem, as he heard Lucy come in just behind Aunt Jo. There was about to be an explosion. A big one.

"Set the table, will you, dear?" Aunt Jo asked Lucy as Chance sauntered into the kitchen and leaned his hip against the counter. Aunt Jo was already bustling about, laying out vegetables to prepare a salad.

They had a system, the three of them. Since Chance was in the kitchen all day, Aunt Jo cooked, Lucy set the table and Chance washed the dishes. A fourth person would break up the whole routine—at least that was how Lucy would see it. It seemed that way to Chance as well.

"Remember to set an extra place," Aunt Jo said over her shoulder.

She didn't see Lucy stiffen, but Chance did, and he knew it was only a matter of seconds before a volcano of emotion erupted in the middle of the kitchen.

He stepped forward to intercept the drama, but not fast enough. Lucy darted under his arm in order to confront Aunt Jo head-on.

"Didn't Dad tell you she can't stay here?" Lucy demanded, her face turning red with anger.

Instead of answering Lucy, Aunt Jo turned to Chance, her hands propped on her ample hips and a determined, fiery light in her eyes. "Did he *what?*"

Chance would have taken a step backward, except the table was in the way. Instead, he assumed a casual posture and shrugged.

"Don't you shrug at me, young man." Aunt Jo shook a finger at him as if he were two years old. Flames of humiliation billowed within him. If Lucy wasn't so distracted, she would have laughed at the scene, and he was certain the beautiful stranger would be doing just that, if she'd been there to witness it. Thankfully, she was still in the bedroom and out of earshot.

At least, he'd *thought* Phoebe was in her room, but he knew he was mistaken when he heard her sudden, shrill intake of breath from behind his shoulder.

Could this day get any worse?

Phoebe had obviously seen, or at least heard, everything—private, family stuff she had no right listening to. That's why he didn't want her in his house—at all.

"I've caused enough trouble here," Phoebe said, stepping forward with her suitcase in her hand. "It's been very nice meeting you all, but I think I should go."

"Good," Lucy declared.

"Lucy!" Chance and Aunt Jo exclaimed at the same time.

Chance narrowed his eyes on his daughter, wondering when she'd become so blatantly disrespectful that she should speak to an adult that way.

Any adult. Even Phoebe Yates. It was bad enough that she talked back to him, but a stranger? He'd taught her better than that.

Or maybe he hadn't, he thought, as guilt sliced through him. He hadn't always been there for his daughter. Not like he should have been.

In any case, it was his responsibility to fix things right now.

"Apologize to Ms. Yates," he ordered, trying to sound stern.

Lucy stared at him as if he'd just told her to stick her hand in a rattlesnake's nest. Her mouth opened and closed without words. Most likely, she'd been about to talk back at him, and then had thought better of it.

Good for her. He wasn't in the mood.

Lucy glanced at Phoebe, then back at Chance, and then she whirled around and ran from the room, wailing dramatically, something about how no one in the house ever cared about her opinion and how she couldn't wait to grow up and get away from there.

Brushing a hand down his face, Chance looked from Aunt Jo to Phoebe, who were both staring back at him expectantly. What were they waiting for him to do?

"Sorry," he muttered. "I really don't know what her problem is."

"I do," Phoebe assured him. She'd dropped her suitcase for a moment when all the ruckus started, but now she picked it back up again. "*I'm* the problem. And I'm out of here. Crisis averted. Take care, now."

"Phoebe, wait." Surprisingly, the words were from his own lips, and the arm that snaked out to grasp Phoebe's suitcase was his.

She stared at him without speaking, but her own grip on her suitcase didn't lessen.

Their gazes locked, his breath hitched in his throat, and for a moment he forgot everything. Why she was here, what they were arguing about. Whether he should make her leave or invite her to stay. Everything.

So he was unprepared when Aunt Jo nudged him from behind. He stepped forward to keep his balance, closing the distance between him and Phoebe to something he wasn't even remotely comfortable with. He panicked.

Physically, he stumbled backward. Verbally, he stumbled ahead. "Aunt Jo has already offered you the hospitality of our home."

"Yes, but you…"

"Agree with her. Frankly, you have nowhere else you can stay. In case you didn't notice, Serendipity isn't exactly a big town."

"But Lucy…" Phoebe started to protest, but Chance held up his hands and cut her off.

"Lucy is thirteen. She'll deal with it."

Phoebe looked hesitant, but Chance thought that was a step up from the determined rejection which had earlier lined her features. At least she was thinking about it.

"You're going to hurt my Aunt Jo's feelings if you go and leave."

While that was true, he immediately regretted

saying so. It was a low blow to play the guilt card, and he knew it. What he *didn't* know was why he was suddenly arguing so fervently for Phoebe to stay, when neither he nor Lucy wanted her there. What kind of nonsense was that?

Because of Aunt Jo, of course. He was doing it for her. What other reason could there be?

"If you're sure…" Phoebe continued to hem and haw, but that half sentence was all Aunt Jo needed to hear to jump into the conversation.

"It's settled, then," she said decisively, and Chance knew in that instant it was. He could see the reluctance on her face slowly morph into acceptance. "Phoebe will stay in this house for the six weeks she is here. This is supposed to be a vacation for her, so let's lose the drama. Chance, be a dear and take Phoebe's suitcase back to the spare room. Phoebe, you can set the table, since I appear to be a little short on help tonight."

Phoebe smiled, looking relieved to have something to do. She had a nice smile, Chance thought, when she wasn't stressing out about something.

Too bad the peace between them wouldn't last. Tomorrow they'd be sharing a kitchen—or at least, she'd be trying to share his kitchen with him.

It wasn't going to work, of course. The folks of Serendipity knew full well why there were no fresh pastries at Cup O' Jo.

Lindsay had been the pastry chef.

Phoebe would be rejected, not just by Lucy, but by the whole town. He almost felt sorry for her.

Almost.

Chapter Three

STATUS UPDATE: PHOEBE YATES: Well, I'm staying—at least for now. I think I can do some good here. At the very least I can fill the empty pastry cases with some of my signature pies and cookies. Yum!

JOSEPHINE HAWKINS MURPHY: Yay! My mouth is watering already.

After a good night's sleep, Phoebe's perspective really *had* changed. Or maybe it was just her usual optimistic nature catching up with yesterday's events. She was grateful for this opportunity, and as she washed up and dressed for the day, she silently thanked God for opening the doors for her to be here in Serendipity.

She wasn't ready to give up yet. She would trust God to smooth away whatever bumps she experienced along the way, though she wasn't foolish enough to think there wouldn't be a few, at least. Probably many more.

But she'd never been one to back down from a challenge, and she wasn't about to start now. This might be a strenuous day, but she had no doubt it would be fulfilling as well, and she couldn't wait to get started.

Her most immediate hurdle, and it was a big one, would be trying to establish a friendly relationship with Chance and his kitchen. The first day on a new job was always a little overwhelming, but Phoebe was certain she could handle it—almost certain, at any rate.

Baking was her passion; it was only a matter of working out the logistical problems. Perhaps Chance wouldn't be so surly now that he'd had a night to think about it.

Yawning, she went searching for a cup of hot coffee. She expected to find Jo, or even Chance, but though it was just after daybreak, there was no one about. Apparently they'd already left for the café, or else they weren't yet up. Phoebe suspected the former, since she knew the café was open for breakfast, so they'd need to get an early start. Her thoughts were confirmed when she found a little note tented in front of the coffeepot on the counter.

The message indicated that she could help herself to anything in the refrigerator, but Phoebe opted for toast. No one had specified what time she should arrive at the café for work—Chance was no doubt still debating whether or not he wanted her there at all—and what with the mixed welcome she'd received yesterday, she'd forgotten to ask.

Presumably, on most mornings, she'd be going into work at daybreak in order to get fresh pastries ready for the breakfast rush—or whatever one would call a slight surge of customers in a small, lazy town like Serendipity. It wasn't like anything in Phoebe's urban experience, but she imagined there would be at least a handful of regulars, since Cup O' Jo was the only restaurant in town that Phoebe knew of. And the café had seemed busy enough yesterday.

The only way she would know for sure was to get on over and see for herself. Washing down the last of her toast with a lukewarm cup of coffee, she fished her car keys from her purse and headed out the door.

Her mind on the day ahead, she didn't immediately see Chance walking along the side of the road, his cowboy hat dipped low against the ever-present west Texas wind. His hands were shoved into the pockets of his trench coat, and he walked with long, purposeful strides.

What was he thinking? The Texas wind was chilly in the morning, and he didn't look like he was enjoying himself. And he *sure* wasn't doing it for the exercise—not with the old, scuffed black cowboy boots he was wearing. Maybe his car was in the shop.

Phoebe pulled to the side of the road and pushed the electric button that rolled down the passenger-side window. He didn't exactly acknowledge her, but she knew he'd seen her, because he froze in place, as still as an ice sculpture—not speaking, and not looking at her.

"Can I give you a lift?" she asked politely.

He took a hasty step backward as if she'd physically pushed him and then turned his head toward her. She could barely see the black of his eyes under the brim of his hat, but his firm, square jaw was taut with tension.

"No," he barked, spinning away from her. As an afterthought, he mumbled, "Thank you," but it didn't sound as if he meant it.

This time it was Phoebe who felt as if *he'd* physically shoved *her,* wounding, if nothing else, her pride.

Chance paced urgently forward, clearly wanting to escape her, but it was easy enough for Phoebe to accelerate the car forward to match his pace as he walked.

What was up with the man? He was going to the same destination as she; why not catch a ride if she'd offered him one? Talk about making no sense, not to mention being downright rude.

As much as she wanted to ask him what his problem was, she knew how *those* words would come out, and it wouldn't be pretty. There was no sense alienating Chance if she didn't have to, given that they'd be working together every day.

At least, not yet. At this rate, she didn't think it would be long before they were at each other's throats—especially in the kitchen.

"Are you sure?" she asked instead. "It's awfully cold outside for you to be walking, and I really wouldn't mind the company."

He stopped again, this time leaning in the window, his features set in stone.

"*I* mind," he said gruffly in that singularly raspy voice of his. "Please. Just leave me alone. I'll meet you at the café."

So much for trying to be friendly.

She shrugged, but Chance didn't see it. He was already walking away from her. Obstinate man.

Yet again, Phoebe wondered what she was getting herself into. Maybe Chance was not sold on their working together, even after having a good night's sleep.

Maybe he hadn't *had* a good night's sleep. He was certainly acting as if he'd woken up on the wrong side of the bed.

Though she didn't want to admit it, his refusal to ride with her felt personal, especially because she couldn't think of a single reason why he would not have accepted her offer. If anything, the two of them having a few minutes to converse on a personal level, before they arrived at the café and had to talk work, would have been a good thing.

Right?

Unless he really hated the thought of being around her, and she thought it was a little early for that, whether she was threatening the use of his kitchen or not. At least he could get to know her first before he decided he wasn't going to like her.

Phoebe arrived at the café a little before seven, and well ahead of Chance. Which was good, since she was still feeling a little confused and put out by his strange actions. She needed a moment to recover and get her bearings before having to face him again.

She had no idea what to say to him, or how to act, given his uncouth behavior, but she knew it would feel awkward to see him again. Praying for guidance, she decided to let it go and take her cue from Chance when the time came. She had other things to think about—nicer things.

It wouldn't be a huge stretch to assume he might be dead-set on giving her trouble, but she wasn't going to let him ruin her day—especially since Jo had realized she was there and was gesturing her inside the café. The welcome smile on the old woman's face and the cheerful twinkle in her eye went a long way toward making Phoebe feel better.

So, for that matter, did her No Attitude T-shirt. As far as Phoebe was concerned, Chance needed to take a clue from the words.

"I'm glad you're here," Jo said, turning the sign on the door from closed to open.

Phoebe was certainly glad *somebody* was happy to see her.

"Most days, we open at seven, though nothing is completely cut-and-dried in this little town. I imagine that after this morning you'll want to get an early start on your daily baking, but I wanted to let you sleep in today, seeing as you just got here, and all."

"Thank you," Phoebe replied, grinning back at Jo. There was no way a person could *not* smile around Jo's bubbly, joyful presence. "I'm usually a morning person, so I'd be perfectly happy to get here a couple of hours early to get fresh pastries in the oven for our breakfast customers."

And to avoid working with Chance, as much as possible, she added mentally, though of course she didn't say it out loud.

"Chance usually comes in at seven?" she asked, hoping she sounded casual, and not like she wanted to avoid the man.

Even though she did. And somehow, Phoebe had the uncomfortable prickling sensation that Jo had picked up on her underlying viewpoint.

"My nephew works his heart out for this café," Jo said, her voice full of affection. "I don't know what I'd do without him. He arrives at seven every morning, six days a week, and doesn't leave until after eight at night. He'd work seven days a week if I'd let him. We're closed on Sundays, so we can all go to church."

Chance was a churchgoing man? From Phoebe's brief but memorable encounters with him, she wouldn't have thought him the type. She wouldn't call his attitude or his actions Christian charity, by any means. But this was a small town. Perhaps things were different here. Maybe everyone attended church as a general rule. Even rude, gruff Chance Hawkins.

"Aunt Jo works harder than I do," came Chance's raspy, rugged-sounding reply from the door. "There's a very good reason her name is on the sign. She's the real heart of this café, and everyone in Serendipity knows it." He ended his statement by giving his Aunt Jo an affectionate buss on the cheek.

Jo smiled in satisfaction.

She wondered how long he'd been standing there listening to their conversation, and whether or not he'd heard her asking questions about him. He couldn't have arrived much earlier, she assured herself, since he'd chosen to *walk* to work.

And where had this tenderhearted man who clearly adored his aunt even come from? It was certainly a night-and-day difference from the man she'd met on the road. Phoebe was floored not only by his words, but by the way his whole demeanor had changed. She was seeing a glimpse of an entirely different man altogether.

At that moment, three older gentlemen dressed

nearly identically in red flannel shirts and denim overalls entered the café and greeted Jo and Chance by name, as friends. Jo introduced Phoebe and then chatted easily with the men as she seated them.

This was what Phoebe was here for. The small-town atmosphere where everybody knew everybody and the pace of life was slow and peaceful.

"Gotta go," Chance said to Phoebe, nodding his head toward the three men. "These guys work the hardware store. They don't just dress alike. They eat alike—every morning. Bacon, hash browns and eggs over easy. A solid country breakfast."

"A heart attack on a plate," Phoebe countered.

He grinned at her. Actually *grinned*.

She crossed her arms, feeling suddenly awkward and out of place just standing there next to the door like she didn't know what she was doing—even if it was true. Jo was still conversing with the men at the table, and Chance was already halfway to the kitchen. Phoebe didn't know if she should stay where she was, or follow Dr. Jekyll and Mr. Hyde into the kitchen.

Chance turned just as he reached the green swinging doors, his brow raised in question.

"After you," he said, stepping back and sweeping his hand toward the doorway.

She didn't know if it was an invitation or an order. Not that it mattered either way. She was still trying to get over his contradictory behavior. Fifteen minutes ago, he wouldn't even ride in her car. Now he was inviting her into his kitchen, his private domain.

Was this some kind of truce?

"We have a problem," he said as soon as he passed through the doors. He hung his hat on the rack, followed by his trench coat, and then wrapped a plain white apron around his waist. When he turned back to her, his stern, hawk-like features and low brow only magnified the intensity of his dark, stormy eyes.

Not a truce, then.

"Okay," she said, willing herself not to respond to Chance's aggressive posture. "I'm listening."

As long as she remained cool and detached, this would be the moment they worked things out. Emotion would only cloud reason. Instead of focusing on the confrontation at hand, she thought about afterward, when she could enjoy her first real day in Serendipity, and maybe even bake something.

She hoped.

"I'm messy," he stated without preamble. "That being said, though it may not appear that way, I have a method to my cooking, a certain way I do things, and I need room. Lots of room."

"Like the whole kitchen. I get it," she said, standing her ground. "I, on the other hand, don't require much room at all to do my baking. I'll need one counter, a place to store my supplies, and shared use of the oven."

Chance's scowl deepened. "Of course you will."

He turned back to the grill, tossing bacon onto the sizzling surface and acting as if they'd never even spoken, or even acknowledging that she was still in the room.

Incensed, Phoebe propped her hands on her hips and glared at him. He didn't see it, but it made her feel better even so.

"So are we going to do this thing, or what? I'm tired of running around the issue without really addressing it. It's your call. Yes or no?"

He turned to her, tongs in midair. "I have breakfast to cook. The bell over the front door just rang, which means we have more customers."

"That's not an answer."

He turned back to the grill. "That's all you're going to get."

Which meant what, exactly?

She had no idea. Clearly he resented her presence in his kitchen, but it seemed to Phoebe that whatever was happening here went a little bit deeper than just a boy not willing to share his toys.

On the other hand, he'd just said *they* had more customers. Was he including her, then?

She stepped to the grill, side by side with Chance, and picked up a spatula.

"I cook a mean fried egg," she offered brightly, feeling tentative in her heart, but making certain it didn't show in her voice.

"Yeah?" he said, sounding at least vaguely interested. "I thought you were some big-time pastry chef who only worked at the most upscale restaurants."

"I still went to cooking school," she said with a chuckle, as she expertly cracked an egg onto the sizzling hot surface of the grill. "I didn't start my career by making wedding cakes and croissants."

"School, huh?" he mused, flipping the hash browns. "Interesting."

Phoebe felt a jolt of triumph at her success. He hadn't pushed her aside when she'd offered to help. That was a good sign. And she'd gotten him talking, and not tuning her out the way he had moments before.

"I even spent some time studying in Paris," she continued. "Popular theory has it that France is where any aspiring chef is supposed to go to learn the secrets of great cooking, so off I went."

"Did you like it?"

"Honestly? It was okay, but there are a lot of other places in the world I'd like to experience."

"Guess I'm not a true aspiring chef, then, at least not by the world's standards. I've never been to school," he admitted as he put the finishing touches on the first three plates, and then slid them out the service window. "And I've definitely never been to Paris."

Too far to walk, Phoebe mused, now finding a little bit of humor in the situation.

"Where did you learn to cook, then?" she asked.

"Right here in this kitchen. My father taught me everything I know."

"Does he still work here?"

"He passed away a few years ago. Mom, too. Now it's just Aunt Jo and me, trying to keep the dream alive. This café has been in our family since the late 1800s, when the original Josephine Hawkins traveled out west as a mail-order bride. It'd be a shame to give it up now, what with all the history, and all."

"How neat that you've learned about your ancestry like that. I don't know a thing about mine. So you have no other family?"

"My wi—Lindsay used to bake the pastries here."

Phoebe heard the catch in his low, raspy voice, and she hadn't missed the way he spoke of his wife in the past tense, either.

Which was interesting, but it didn't really tell her anything. A bad divorce could be almost as painful as a spouse dying. Whatever had happened between Chance and Lindsay, it was obviously still a fresh wound, and she wasn't sure she should prod any further into that part of his personal life on such short acquaintance.

She was still debating about whether or not to ask more about his wife when Jo entered the room, a pained expression on her face. She wobbled a little bit, looking faint, and was breathing heavily.

Both Phoebe and Chance rushed to her side, easing

her into the single chair in the kitchen. Phoebe was concerned with how peaked she looked. She tried to gauge what was wrong with the woman, but couldn't tell, not having much experience with this sort of thing. She hoped it wasn't a stroke or a heart attack.

"Is it your hip again?" Chance asked, crouching before the old woman.

Jo nodded. "Blasted thing is really acting up on me today."

"If you'd just listen to the doctor…" said Chance compassionately.

"The *doctor* wants me to have surgery," Jo snapped. "Replacing the hip God gave me with steel rods. I don't think so. Not going to happen."

Phoebe was so relieved that it wasn't something life-threatening that she almost chuckled at Jo's spunky attitude, but she didn't. It might just be Jo's hip, but from the expression on Chance's face, the situation was still serious.

"Did you take your pain meds, at least?" Chance asked, laying a comforting hand on Jo's shoulder.

"You know that medicine makes me loopy," she replied, making it sound like a chastisement. "I've got customers out there expecting their coffee."

"I'll call Shelley and see if she can come in to help you," Chance offered, standing.

Jo's hand snaked out, grasping Chance by the wrist and pulling him back.

"You'll do no such thing. This is Shelley's only

day off this week. She's already working more than is proper. I'll not have her take over for me."

Privately, Phoebe wondered why Jo didn't just hire more help, but now was not the time to ask such a question. Whatever the reason, Jo clearly would not be able to continue working, no matter how she felt about it.

Phoebe met Chance's dark, concerned gaze over the top of Jo's head.

"I'm on it," she declared, plucking the pad and pencil from Jo's hand. Jo tried to protest, but Phoebe wouldn't even think of it.

"You," she said in a no-nonsense tone as she gestured at Jo, "go home and get some rest.

"And you," she said to Chance with an authoritative smile, "keep cooking up those good country meals. Show me what you can do with that grill. Who knows? Maybe Serendipity will turn out to be the next Paris."

Chapter Four

STATUS UPDATE: PHOEBE YATES: No offense to @JosephineHawkinsMurphy, but the guy I'm working with here at the café isn't exactly the easiest person to get along with. I think the Lord is trying to test my patience.

JOSEPHINE HAWKINS MURPHY: None taken, dear. I'm the first to admit my nephew can be difficult. But I think if anyone can reach him, it's you.

Chance's head was spinning. Unconsciously, he reached for the counter to keep himself upright—at least physically. Mentally he wasn't so sure.

Phoebe had taken over running the café as if she'd been working at Cup O' Jo all her life. A complete stranger to all of them, she'd gently but firmly laid down the law where Aunt Jo and her aching hip was concerned.

And Aunt Jo had listened to her!

This very moment, Aunt Jo and her beloved Bessie the truck were on their way back to the house. She had even caved in to Phoebe's insistence that she go straight to bed to rest. Chance couldn't think of one other instance where Aunt Jo had followed someone else's orders. Not even her husband, Chance's Uncle Paul, had been able to bend her to his way of thinking unless and until she was ready to go there on her own.

While Chance had heard Phoebe threaten to check on Aunt Jo when they arrived home, he couldn't believe that was the reason the older woman had become so suddenly complacent and mild, either. He'd made enough threats of his own over the years, which Aunt Jo had always completely ignored.

Somehow, the unaccounted for change in the situation had something to do with Phoebe herself. Chance couldn't put his finger on what exactly *it* was, only that it was there. One thing was certain— she had a strong, vibrant personality, which was probably part of the reason she had risen so high in her chosen career—that, and the fact that she presumably baked well. The jury was still out on that one, since he hadn't tasted her cooking yet.

But back to the point, Aunt Jo was no lame duck. Chance could have pleaded and pressured her all day, and Aunt Jo wouldn't have budged an inch. She wouldn't have taken the time to rest in his *kitchen*, never mind at home.

Chance scoffed and shook his head. Phoebe Yates definitely had a way about her. He would have to be on his guard when she was around.

Curious as to how she was faring as a waitress, he stood to one side of the order window and peered out, careful not to be seen. He felt both conspicuous and a little silly. What did it matter if she saw him looking at her?

But as ridiculous as it might be, it did matter. He didn't want her to think he was interested in what she was doing, even if he was.

And why shouldn't he be? This was his café—sort of. Or at least it would be, someday. He had a right to see how Phoebe was treating his customers.

More than that, he wanted to see how the customers were taking to her. The people of Serendipity were friendly folk, but Chance knew they would be wondering about this newcomer to town, the woman who would be taking over the baking at Cup O' Jo.

Taking over Lindsay's job.

He hissed as the breath left his lungs. That punched-in-the-gut feeling never quite went away. It never stopped hurting. Ever.

Phoebe was hovering near the table where the three old men from the hardware store had finished eating and were preparing to leave. She leaned forward and said something Chance couldn't hear. The men laughed in unison.

With a pencil alternately tucked behind her ear and in her hand, she moved from one table to another, scribbling on her pad. When she had visited four tables, she approached the order window.

"It's about time," he said gruffly. "I was beginning to wonder if you'd forgotten that I need the orders to cook the food."

She chuckled, not at all the response he'd anticipated. She didn't seem to let anything get to her at all, most especially his perpetually bad mood.

"Hardly," she said, tearing off four sheets of orders and sliding them across the counter toward him. Each was written in a bold, round script. "I just wanted to see if you could multitask."

Chance grinned. He couldn't seem to help himself. "Just watch me."

Phoebe went back to order-taking and Chance turned his attention to the grill with a sense of determination he hadn't felt in ages.

He'd show her how well he could multitask.

A half an hour passed with hardly a word between them as they worked through the breakfast crowd. It wasn't easy to keep his mind on his work with her distracting him the way she was—smiling at him every time she slid orders across the counter or picked up food. Couldn't she just do her work without being so unendingly cheerful?

He was so lost in his own musings that he was startled when he suddenly felt a hand on his shoulder. He jumped back and the yolk of the egg he was frying broke and spread into a yellow mess all over the grill.

"Hey, lady," he complained curtly. "Hasn't anyone ever taught you that it's not a good idea to sneak up on a person that way?" He scooped up the ruined egg with his spatula and flipped it into the trash, then turned to face her.

"Sorry." She smiled again—or maybe the grin had never left her face at all. Annoying woman.

And she definitely didn't sound *sorry*. Or look it, for that matter. She was clearly amused, though she did look a little frayed at the edges. But then, who wouldn't be, having been tossed into waitressing a busy breakfast lot? Actually, she'd done a remarkable job, especially considering that he was sure waiting tables wasn't in her usual job description. It was a role quite beneath her renowned chef status, and yet she'd handled herself with both grace and efficiency.

"I just wanted to ask you where the bussing tub might be. There are quite a few tables that I need to clean up before the lunch rush hits."

"Don't worry about it," he said with a shrug. "I'll get to it. This is probably the last breakfast order— once I fry up a new egg, that is."

He probably should have felt bad for teasing her, but the priceless look on her face was worth it—her widened hazel eyes and the way her full lips made a silent *O*. But just as quickly her expression turned into a mock glare.

"You aren't going to let me forget about that, are you?" she asked, perching her hands on her hips.

His grin widened. "I'll see how much mileage I can get out of it first." He gestured to the chair. "Why don't you sit down and rest your feet for a moment while I get this last order done? Then I'll get those tables bussed."

She looked genuinely surprised, maybe even offended, though at what he could not say. Her hazel eyes took on the glitter of determination and she shook her head.

"Just point the way to the bussing tub, please," she insisted.

He shrugged. "Your call. Don't say I didn't offer. You know your feet are going to be killing you by the end of the day, what with you wearing those heels and all."

"Believe me, long hours on my feet is something I'm well acquainted with, heels or no heels. The tub?"

"Under the sink."

He realized there was no sense arguing with her. The woman was as stubborn as a mule on a hot day.

But there was something intriguing about a world-renowned chef pulling a battered gray bussing tub from under the sink and then heading out to clear the tables at some hole-in-the-wall café in the middle of nowhere. She wasn't full of herself at all, not like he would have expected her to be.

She just saw what needed to be done and did it—without a word of complaint, and without calling undue attention to herself.

"You're different than I thought you'd be," he admitted as she returned to the kitchen with a tub full of dirty plates and utensils. He took the tub from her and put it next to the sinks.

"How so?" she asked, stepping up beside him and filling the first sink with hot, sudsy water and a drop of bleach, as all good dishwashers knew to do. Apparently her expertise in the kitchen didn't begin and end with pastries.

He took her gently by the shoulders and moved her in front of the second sink, stepping into the first position himself.

"I'll wash, you rinse," he stated, scooping up a handful of plates and submerging them in the water.

"Okay," she agreed easily, reaching for the sprayer. "But you still haven't told me just what you expected."

"I didn't mean that in a bad way." He stopped himself before he could spout any more untruths. "Okay, maybe I did. I'm a little cynical, if you haven't already noticed."

"A little?"

He shrugged. He'd already admitted too much.

What was it about this woman that made him open his mouth and insert both feet?

She stared at him for a moment, her head tipped to one side and a thoughtful look on her face. It didn't take him long to feel uncomfortable under her intense scrutiny.

"What?" he asked when he couldn't stand her staring at him anymore.

"Nothing," she replied, turning back to the dishes. "I won't pry."

"Humph," he answered. In his experience, *prying* and *women* went together like hotcakes and syrup. "Well, good."

"Good," she agreed with a nod. "Now, tell me what kind of person you thought I was going to be."

He wished he'd never made that comment in the first place. He really didn't want to elaborate on the subject, but he had the distinct impression she wasn't going to let the subject drop.

At least the heat was off of him.

For now.

Somehow, he didn't think her discretion regarding his personal affairs would last very long. Even if she wasn't actively looking for information on the subject, she was bound to hear the people in town talking about him, and then she'd wonder about him all the more. And then she'd ask. And he didn't want to talk about it.

He wished he could come up with some way to

divert her—at least for now. Too bad for him that every thought in his head was either defensive or just plain lame.

"All I meant was that you're some highfalutin pastry chef with a name every cook worth his salt has heard about." That wasn't quite how he wanted to word it, but there was no turning back now.

"Have you? Heard of me, that is."

How had she twisted his words around again? That she was *right* only made it worse. He gave a clipped nod.

She grinned, clearly pleased that she'd made some sort of impression on him even before she'd ever arrived in this little town.

"And yet here you are waitressing tables in this rickety old shack of a café," he continued. "You weren't even above bussing dirty tables when the need arose."

"Why would I be?" she demanded, sounding genuinely offended. "I'm just as much a human being as you are, thank you very much."

With that, she reached out and sharply pinched his shoulder between her thumb and forefinger.

"Ow!" he complained, rubbing his arm with his palm. "What was that for?"

"Just making sure *you* are human."

"Most people in this town think that's up for debate," he muttered.

"Well, I can see why, if you won't even take a ride

to work when one is offered to you. In good faith, I might add."

Chance had been enjoying their banter—having a surprisingly good time, in truth, but her words instantly made him tunnel in on himself, back into that pitch-black cavern where he usually lived.

He knew his sudden change in demeanor wasn't lost on Phoebe.

"I've said the wrong thing, haven't I?" Her soft, compassionate tone touched him more even than her words did—right to his heart.

Chance swallowed against the burn in his throat and shook his head, knowing—and fully aware that she knew—that he was denying the truth. She had said *exactly* the wrong thing.

"I'm sorry," she apologized softly.

"For what?"

"For whatever I just said that caused you pain," she answered.

"It's nothing."

"If you say so." She turned the sprayer on and started rinsing dishes faster than Chance could wash them. Clearly she was giving him a moment to regroup, which was kind of her. It was an uneasy silence, but Chance didn't know what to say to fill the empty air, so he said nothing.

When the dishes were done, Phoebe folded napkins while Chance filled the salt and pepper shakers.

"You met a lot of new people today," he said,

desperately searching for some neutral ground on which they could field a conversation. Phoebe hadn't said a word in fifteen minutes, and it was starting to bother him. "What did you think of the residents of Serendipity? They're a colorful bunch, aren't they?"

"They're wonderful," she said after a long pause.

"They sure are. Many of the folks here in town visit the café at least once a day. Some even more than that. Maybe when the lunch crowd arrives I can give you a better idea of who's who."

"That would be nice. Getting thrown into waitressing on my first day is probably a better way for me to meet the people of Serendipity than simply working back in the kitchen would have been."

"Can't hurt," he agreed. "But I can do one better than that."

"Which would be?"

"A friend I went to school with, Cody Sparks, and his family are having an old-fashioned country barn-raising on Saturday. It's an opportunity for folks around town to help them out. Unfortunately, a tornado took out their old one earlier this month."

"How awful for them," she said sincerely. "Was anyone hurt?"

"Not a one of them. Even the animals got out all right. If you ask me, their old barn was an eyesore to begin with. It needed to be replaced, anyway. Now it's just sooner, rather than later."

"That's a good attitude," she commented softly.

"Folks around here tend to think calamities like this one are simply a God-given opportunity to start over and make things better."

"I can't even imagine." Her voice trailed off.

He shrugged. In Serendipity, that's just the way things were done—and had always been done. It was a mind-set built on many generations of tough western folk.

He glanced at her when she didn't speak further. She was looking at him like she had a question but was hesitant to ask. Her full lips were twisted and her brow was low. On another woman, that might not have been the most attractive expression. On Phoebe, it was endearing.

"What?" he queried.

"I know I'm going to sound like an idiot, but exactly what is a barn-raising?"

"You're not an idiot," he assured her. "Just a city girl. A barn-raising is just what it sounds like. All the neighbors will be there. Everyone brings food to share, and we all pitch in and build a barn in one day."

"It sounds—intriguing," Phoebe admitted.

"I wasn't going to go, but Lucy's been bugging me about it, and I think it would do us all some good."

Truth be told, it was going to be sheer agony for him. In the past, he'd purposefully avoided just such situations, and for a very good reason. He didn't want the neighbors to talk any more than they already did, even if he told himself it didn't matter what people thought.

Lindsay had loved social situations, and when she was alive he'd attended community events for her sake. As for himself, he'd always leaned on the anti-social, solitary side of the fence. He didn't need a lot of people around him to make his life full.

At one time, all he'd needed was Lindsay, and then Lucy, when she'd come along. Aunt Jo had always been there for him as well. But how Phoebe had managed to get her foot in the door of his insignificant world after such a short acquaintance was beyond him. He'd rather think about the barn-raising.

This would be painful, maybe excruciatingly so, for him, on any number of levels.

But it *would* be good for Phoebe. And he had no doubt it would be good for Lucy.

Maybe, Lord willing, it would be good for Phoebe and Lucy together. He could only hope.

He knew he'd set a bad example for Lucy where Phoebe was concerned. He hadn't nipped Lucy's bad attitude in the bud—in fact, in his own way he'd contributed to it.

Now he had to fix the problems he'd created. And what better way to do that than to spend a whole day playing and working together?

Chapter Five

STATUS UPDATE: PHOEBE YATES: I know there are plenty of books out there on how to relate to men, but are there any on how to deal with men who have teenage daughters who can't stand to be in the same room with you?

JOSEPHINE HAWKINS MURPHY: Don't worry your pretty little head, dear. She'll warm up to you. Mark my words.

Phoebe surreptitiously watched as Chance silently bundled up in his trench coat, adjusted the black bandana around his neck and planted his cowboy hat on his head. He gestured her out of the now-closed café and locked the door behind them, walked her to her car, and then turned and started walking down the road without a single word to her.

For about two seconds, she tossed around the idea of offering him a ride once again, but in the end she simply drove right past him and back to the house they now shared. If he had wanted her to give him a lift home, he would have asked. One deliberate and painful rejection a day was quite enough for her, thank you.

At least she could be thankful that she and Chance were on better terms than they had been this morning. Or at least she hoped they were. From her perspective, they had worked well together, though that might have been because she hadn't actually been underfoot in his kitchen. That part of the equation still remained to be worked out.

But he *had* invited her to join the Hawkins family for that barn-raising thing. That had to count for something.

She was looking forward to participating in this homemade slice of small-town America—and not only for the reasons she'd have expected, why she'd come to Serendipity in the first place. At this point, she was equally excited about the prospect of spending quality time with Chance and his family as she was experiencing the uniquely branded Serendipity to its fullest.

She wanted to get to know Chance better on a personal level, and this seemed as good a way as any. But more important was her relationship—or lack of one—with Lucy. If some dynamic didn't change at the house, it was going to be a long six weeks.

From the very first moment, Jo had welcomed her with open arms, treating her as one of the family.

Chance was a harder nut to crack. She'd promised Chance she wouldn't pry, and she hadn't, but last night when she and Jo were chatting, Jo had filled her in on the details of Chance's life that Phoebe had been missing—the heartrending story of how Lindsay had died in some sort of car accident four years ago. Jo didn't go into great detail, but she didn't need to. It didn't take a rocket scientist to realize the man was still grieving for his wife.

And while Phoebe had seen small glimpses of warmth and kindness behind the gruff, churlish exterior he presented to the world, most off the time he shut himself away behind that dark, brooding exterior. It wouldn't be an easy task to successfully draw him out from behind the mental barrier he'd created between them.

And then there was Lucy—truly problematic, as Phoebe had admittedly little experience with teenage girls.

Okay, *none,* she mentally acknowledged, though she vaguely remembered the confusing mix of polar emotions she'd struggled with at Lucy's age. Having developed a little later than some of her peers, she recalled how gawky and gangly her tall, reed-thin figure had made her feel. She'd become interested in boys about that time as well, even if they hadn't necessarily wanted anything to do with her.

She'd been a figurative fish out of water, wildly flapping her tail in order to get back into the ocean and fit into her own school of fish. Thirteen wasn't an easy age to be for a girl.

Was that how Lucy felt?

As if drawn by her thoughts, Lucy was waiting on the front porch as Phoebe pulled into the long driveway. She was sitting on the bottom stairs, holding a branch in her hand. From what Phoebe could see, she appeared to be writing something in the dirt between her booted feet.

Lucy looked up when the car door slammed and glared in Phoebe's direction. There was bound to be a confrontation, and Phoebe's head was suddenly beginning to throb with a tension headache. There was a lot riding on her being able to make peace with the girl.

Like having the remote possibility of enjoying her time in Serendipity. Like any opportunity to live peacefully in this new and interesting environment. This whole adventure was *way* more complicated than she'd imagined it would be.

"Hi, Lucy," Phoebe called in her friendliest tone of voice. "Are you waiting for your dad? He was right behind me when we left. I'm sure he'll be home in just a few minutes."

Lucy stood and crossed her arms. Her jaw was

clenched and Phoebe thought perhaps the girl's eyes were glistening with tears.

Phoebe winced. Was she the cause of all this? The last thing she wanted to do was make an already bad situation even worse.

"What are you drawing there?" she asked as she approached the porch, pointing to the dirt at Lucy's feet.

Lucy's cheeks immediately stained cherry-red—from embarrassment or anger. Maybe it was a little of both. She kicked at the dirt, but not before Phoebe had read what she'd written.

Brian.

Phoebe smiled to herself. She had a good notion of what Lucy had been doing—daydreaming about the boy she liked. How many times had a teenage Phoebe scribbled the name of her current crush onto the front of a notebook or into the sand on the beach?

Phoebe didn't remark on it, but she filed the knowledge away for the future. Lucy wasn't used to having a woman around, other than her Aunt Jo, who clearly had her hands full just running the café. Maybe Lucy could use another female role model in her life.

If Phoebe could somehow gain Lucy's trust...

"Why do you have to stay in this house?" Lucy demanded, every bit as forthright as her exasperating father. "We don't want you here."

The girl's scowl deepened and her lips turned

down at the corners. She thought it was actually kind of a cute expression, were it not for the fact that Lucy was so earnest and the look in question was directed at Phoebe.

"Your Aunt Jo has asked me to stay here as her guest," Phoebe explained softly, though she knew Lucy was already aware of the arrangement.

Lucy shook her head. "It's not her house. It's my dad's house, and my house, and we don't want you here."

"I'm sorry, Lucy, but it's not just your aunt's idea anymore. Your dad has asked me to stay, and I've accepted. I hope we can be friends." Phoebe made a placating gesture with her arms.

"No way," Lucy responded brusquely. "I will never be friends with you."

The girl was nothing if not straightforward to the point of being rude—much like her father, Phoebe thought. As the old saying went, the apple hadn't fallen far from the tree. The girl might look like her mother, but she definitely had her father's curt personality. Phoebe couldn't help but feel a little hurt and rejected by the girl's response.

It had been a long day.

"Well, it's your call," Phoebe offered, "but no matter how you feel about me, I would like to be your friend. If you change your mind, you know where to find me."

"I'm not going to change my mind." Lucy spun

around and stomped up the wooden stairs and into the house, leaving a literal trail of dust behind her.

Phoebe fanned the grime away from her face and coughed repeatedly.

"That went well," she muttered to herself.

Deciding she would wait outside until Chance got home to ask him how he thought it best for her to approach Lucy, she took the girl's spot on the bottom step of the porch and picked up the branch the girl had discarded.

It wasn't long before her mind was a million miles away as she appraised and discarded various solutions to effectively deal with the teenage girl and that ruggedly handsome, annoyingly standoffish and confusing father of hers.

"Hey, there." Chance's deep, raspy voice pierced into her thoughts and his shadow loomed over her. She jumped to her feet, placing a hand over her racing heart.

"You startled me," she said, her words hovering somewhere between an explanation and an accusation.

"Yeah, I can see that." He tipped his hat to her with his thumb and index finger, but he didn't apologize.

Her lungs burned as she inhaled and exhaled. "I was just thinking about things."

"Uh-huh," he acknowledged gruffly. "And drawing in the dirt." He pointed to the ground at her feet.

Her gaze unthinkingly followed to where he had

pointed, expecting to see nothing out of sorts. She might have been doodling while she was thinking, but she'd never been an artist, at least not the kind who was able to draw more than a crude stick figure.

But, she realized in horror as she stared down at her handiwork, she hadn't been drawing images at all.

She'd been writing.

Chance's name. More than once.

Her heart slammed into her head and heat instantly diffused her cheeks. She lurched forward, stirring the dirt with both feel, creating a cloud of dust that would have suffocated her, had she not been choking already.

There was no possibility whatsoever that Chance could not have seen what she'd written, although there were any number of appalling ways he could interpret—or rather, *misinterpret* the words.

Her gaze flashed to his, but there was nothing in his expression to indicate he'd seen what she had written. No smile hovered on those masculine lips—no frown, either, for that matter. There was no amused gleam in his eyes, nor was there annoyance.

In fact, she couldn't read him at all, which was in its own way worse than knowing what he was thinking. His hard-planed face gave nothing away.

"What are you doing out here?" he asked in a neutral, unnaturally conversational tone.

Not what you're thinking, she wanted to reply,

but of course she didn't. Granted, she didn't exactly know what he was thinking, but whatever it was, it couldn't be good for her. She'd rather not call attention to herself if it could be avoided.

"Did Lucy lock you out?" he suggested with a wink, one side of his lips tugging upward.

"No," Phoebe immediately replied, glad she had finally found her voice. "At least, I don't think she did. I haven't actually tried the door, but I guess I wouldn't be surprised if I couldn't open it. She dashed inside a few minutes ago—anything to get away from me, if I'm not mistaken."

"You've seen her, then."

Phoebe nodded.

"I take it that didn't go well?"

"No," she agreed. "It didn't. Which is why I was waiting out here for you to get home, actually."

"So I can protect you from my feral daughter?"

"I think I can hold my own," she assured him wryly. "But I do think we should talk about how you think I should best handle this. You know your daughter much better than I do. Is there something I can do to reduce her apprehension?"

"Yeah, about that…"

"Yes?"

His hands jammed into the pockets of his trench coat, he looked at the ground and stirred the dirt around with the tip of his boot for a moment before continuing. "I'm sorry for the way Lucy's been treating you."

Phoebe didn't know what she had expected him to say, but an apology seemed out of character for him. Of course, he was apologizing for his daughter and had not mentioned his own actions at all, though he'd been at least as rude to her as Lucy had.

Lucy's reaction she could understand, and even, on some level, relate to.

Chance? Not so much.

"You have to understand that for the past four years it's just been the two of us and Aunt Jo," he explained in that low, throaty voice of his. This time he didn't sound gruff; rather, it seemed to Phoebe that he was attempting to hold his emotions in check.

What a terrible tragedy for anyone to face. Phoebe couldn't help but feel for him—for both of them. She nodded. "I imagine she misses her mother terribly."

"Yes," Chance agreed, momentarily dropping his gaze. Clearly Lucy was not the only one who missed Lindsay. It was obviously a difficult subject for Chance to talk about.

"She is very protective of you."

"Overprotective, you mean." Chance lifted his hat and combed his long, tapered fingers through his curly black hair. They were chef's hands, Phoebe thought, capable, in the right conditions, of the creation of a culinary masterpiece.

He definitely had the mind for it. The circumstances were another thing entirely. Phoebe was pretty sure Cup O' Jo, with its usual down-home customers ordering ordinary country fare, was not the place to find out just how capable Chance was in the kitchen.

Lucy, on the other hand…

"Does Lucy cook?" she asked as a new idea suddenly occurred to her. Maybe baking was something they could do together, a way for Phoebe to share her passion with the girl.

Chance shook his head. "She used to bake with her mother all the time, but now she has—" he paused, his mouth pulling to one side as he considered his next words "—lost interest in it."

Cooking was out, then. Phoebe knew better than to try to pursue such a lead, even if it happened to be her specialty. Lucy obviously connected baking to her mother. Phoebe wouldn't even want to try to fill those shoes.

"I want to get along with Lucy," Phoebe offered, bemused and unsettled. She wasn't any closer to figuring out how she was going to live with the Hawkins family than she had been when she'd walked in the door last evening. "Frankly, I just don't know how that's going to happen."

Chance's brow lowered over obsidian eyes as he blew out a low, frustrated breath. Clearly he shared Phoebe's concerns regarding Lucy.

"Just give her some time," he suggested softly after some time, rhythmically tapping his hat against his leg. "Hopefully she'll come around on her own."

Phoebe privately agreed with Chance and silently lifted her concerns in prayer. God was the One who could change people's hearts. For all their sakes, they needed to learn to live together, or something would have to give.

That, Phoebe knew, would be her, and now she wasn't in such a hurry to leave. Hopefully, her adventure here was just beginning.

STATUS UPDATE: PHOEBE YATES: I've feasted on the highest quality gourmet foods from all around the world—New York, France, Italy. But there's something to be said for plain old-country cooking. The beef roast, fried potatoes and steamed broccoli we had for supper was spectacular.

JOSEPHINE HAWKINS MURPHY: Why thank you, dear. I'll have to share the recipe with you.

Little had been said over dinner. Aunt Jo chattered merrily about all the latest town gossip and didn't seem to notice that no one else at the table appeared to be joining in.

Or maybe, Chance thought, he wasn't giving his

aunt enough credit. More than likely Aunt Jo knew exactly what was going on and was filling in the silent void with words so that no one else would have to speak unless they wanted to.

As for Chance, he didn't have anything to say.

Phoebe was obviously deep in thought—probably musing over her confrontation with his irrational daughter. Lucy was using her fork to push her food around her plate without really eating anything. If she sulked any deeper her bottom lip would be dragging on the ground.

Chance knew he should be thinking about how to ease the tension between Phoebe and his daughter, but to his own dismay, his mind kept wandering in one direction.

Phoebe.

Not Lucy and Phoebe. Just Phoebe.

He couldn't seem to get her out of his mind. She'd walked into his life in the worst way, and yet here he was, experiencing feelings he'd thought had died forever when he'd buried Lindsay.

He told himself—repeatedly—that it was just a surface attraction. Phoebe was a pretty woman with shiny chestnut hair and brilliant hazel eyes. And though their careers had taken entirely different paths, they both shared a devotion of the culinary arts. That had to count for something in explaining his irrational, doomed-to-an-enormous-train-wreck of thought.

He knew the exact second when his perspective had changed—when he had seen his own name scribbled in the dirt. *Phoebe's* handiwork.

It shouldn't have meant anything to him, but in that one moment, his heart had jammed into his throat so hard he couldn't breathe and his pulse started racing. It was more than a simple shock, he acknowledged silently. It was a bombshell—a horde of mixed emotions he didn't even want to put a name to, much less explore.

And yet, when he looked into those hazel eyes…

"So, Lucy," he said, his raspy voice slicing through the silence like a dull-edged knife. "I have a surprise for you."

Lucy's gaze flung out in Phoebe's direction before settling on her father. "She's leaving?"

"That's enough, young lady," Chance reprimanded sharply, his brow furrowing.

Chance groaned softly. Was it any wonder Lucy's barrage of callous words were striking their target? Lucy wouldn't let up on the poor woman even for a moment. And at the end of the day, it was his fault.

"Lucy. It's not like you to be mean. Apologize to Ms. Yates."

"It's Phoebe, please," Phoebe inserted.

Lucy dropped her gaze from Chance's scowl, but even still she refused to speak.

"Now," he insisted.

"Sorry," the girl mumbled under her breath. She

didn't look sorry—or sound it, for that matter. In fact, it was the least sincere apology Chance had ever heard in his life. That said, he doubted he'd get anything better from her, even if he forced the issue.

Lucy stood up, glaring at Phoebe and absolutely refusing to look at Chance.

"May I be excused, please?" she asked in a bitter tone of voice that set Chance's teeth on edge.

"No, you may not," he said sternly. "Now sit down."

Phoebe laid a restraining hand on his arm and shook her head, all in one graceful, fluid motion performed so judiciously that Lucy didn't even see it— which was good, because Chance knew good and well that his daughter would be furious with such a gesture, even if it was for her benefit.

In any case, Chance got the message, and the pleading look Phoebe flashed him confirmed his thoughts. He'd pushed enough for one night. Anything else he might try would likely do more damage than good, not only to Lucy, but to Phoebe, as well.

Aunt Jo, sitting at the head of the table, nodded in silent agreement. Having lived at the house since Lindsay died, she knew more about how his daughter ticked than anyone. He greatly valued her good opinion.

It didn't sit right with him to lose a battle of wills, especially against Lucy, but he consoled himself by remembering that one single battle did not win a war.

And he *would* win the war.

He didn't know how he would do it, but he was resolved to make things right between Lucy and Phoebe. It was becoming personal now.

"Don't you even want to know what your surprise is?" he asked, deliberately trying to shift Lucy's focus to a more pleasant topic.

"Depends on what it is," she answered cautiously, looking from Chance to Phoebe and back.

"Well, I've been thinking," Chance started, but he paused when Lucy rolled her eyes.

Beside him, Phoebe chuckled. He lifted an eyebrow at her. A joke at his expense wasn't exactly what he'd had in mind to bring the two females together on one side.

Make that *three* females. Aunt Jo was laughing, too.

"I've been thinking," he repeated in a louder, firmer tone of voice, "that it might be fun for us to go to the Sparkses' barn-raising next weekend."

"Really?" Lucy's face lit up from the upward curve of her lips to her glowing green eyes. Chance thought it might have been worth it to go to the barn-raising just to see the smile on his daughter's face. Why hadn't he realized that before?

Unfortunately, he should have enjoyed that short flash of enjoyment while it lasted, for a moment later Lucy's smile faded.

"Us?" she queried irately.

Chance sighed heavily. "Yes, us. You, me, Aunt Jo and Phoebe."

"Why does she have to come?" Lucy asked, pointing an accusatory finger at Phoebe.

"Do you *really* want to go there?" he retorted crisply. Exasperating child.

Lucy shrugged, but she didn't push the issue. "Can I *please* be excused now? I can't wait to text all my friends and let them know I'm coming."

He chuckled. "Two more bites of broccoli first."

"Dad," she complained, though this time without the sting in her tone, "I'm not two."

"No, you're not," Chance agreed. "But you still have to eat your vegetables."

Lucy sighed dramatically and popped two broccoli flowerets into her mouth. "Now?"

"Go."

Lucy was out of the room almost before he'd spoken the single syllable. He shook his head as he watched her go.

"It's just a barn-raising," he mused softly to no one in particular.

Aunt Jo chuckled. "Are you so far over the hill that you don't remember what it's like to be a teenager at a barn-raising?"

Chance scowled and shook his head. "That's different. She's a girl."

Phoebe's pleasant-voiced laughter joined in with Aunt Jo's. "You just keep telling yourself that."

"What's that supposed to mean?" His gaze traveled

from woman to woman, both of whom were looking quite smug, like they knew something he didn't.

"You've buried your head in the sand, dear," Aunt Jo offered. "Quite deeply, I believe. You can't possibly *not* have noticed how Lucy is blooming into a young lady. Let's not forget she's a teenager now."

"She's not *blooming*," he said, though his denial obviously fell on deaf ears.

"What grade is she in?" Phoebe queried.

"She just finished seventh."

"I started liking boys when I was in the seventh grade," Phoebe said thoughtfully. Or maybe she was poking fun at him. He couldn't tell.

"Boys?" This was not helpful. "If I see a boy so much as looking at my daughter during this barn-raising, I'll string him up by his ears."

Phoebe laughed. "Why does that not surprise me? I totally picture you as the type of dad who will meet Lucy's dates at the door with a baseball bat in your hand."

"Lucy is not dating until she is thirty," he pronounced firmly. End of subject.

"I'm sure she'll be sorry to hear that, Chance, dear," Aunt Jo said with humor lacing her voice. "Now why don't you go finish the chores in the barn while Phoebe and I wash these dishes up?"

He started to protest. He always finished the chores in the barn before supper, as Aunt Jo knew well. It was usually his job to wash the dinner dishes.

But that wasn't the point, now was it?

He might be a guy, but he wasn't that thickheaded. Clearly, the two of them wanted him out of the way, for who knew what reason. Probably to talk behind his back, woman to woman or some such nonsense. The addition of Phoebe to the household had definitely turned Chance's world on its axis.

There were far too many females around here. He was surrounded by them on all sides, and he'd be toast if and when they decided to gang up on him.

This could *not* be good.

He whistled for his Heinz 57 shepherd mix named King—a *male,* thankfully—and headed out for the barn. At least he'd have a little peace and quiet out there—if he could get Phoebe out of his head.

Not likely, but he would try.

Chapter Six

STATUS UPDATE: PHOEBE YATES: What do you wear to an old-fashioned country barn-raising? I'm going to have the opportunity to meet a lot of the people here in Serendipity, more even than I've seen at the café—if I can figure out what to wear.

Phoebe had had a good chat with Jo while they finished the dishes. As always, the older woman had made her smile, despite all the mixed emotions she was feeling at the moment. Now back in her bedroom, she had time to mull over what Jo had said, or at least implied.

According to Jo, things were going even better than she had planned. Phoebe didn't know exactly what those *things* were that Jo was hinting at, and she wasn't even sure she wanted to find out.

Even if she knew, she would probably have to

disagree. Whatever headway she'd made with Chance was that much farther back she'd gone with Lucy.

The girl hated her—and in no uncertain terms, wanted her gone.

Rejection was rejection, and it stung, even if it came from a thirteen-year-old girl. Maybe *especially* because it came from a thirteen-year-old girl. Chance's daughter.

Even so, Phoebe couldn't help but feel sorry for Lucy. Her mother's death had taken an enormous toll on the girl, more so perhaps than anyone had realized. And though Chance clearly loved his daughter and tried his best, Lucy was floundering emotionally. It had taken Phoebe coming into the household and disrupting the status quo to raise up the emotional issues Lucy clearly hadn't dealt with.

Phoebe knew she needed to spend extra time in prayer for the whole Hawkins family. She'd learned over the years that prayer was the first line of defense. She knew now that she was not going to leave, even though on the surface it appeared she was making things more difficult for Lucy. Instead, she would do whatever she could to reach out to Lucy— even if she was rejected.

Repeatedly.

This last resolution was not only for Lucy's sake, but for Chance, as well. If there was any way she could ease the pain she occasionally glimpsed in Chance's dark gaze, she wanted to do it. She'd somehow become personally invested in the man, maybe from the first moment she'd walked into his kitchen and had seen him glaring back at her, challenging her.

She hadn't anticipated becoming emotionally entangled with the Hawkins family, and yet here she was, only the second day into her vacation, neck-deep in family drama.

A smart woman might walk away. Instead, Phoebe's heart urged her to step forward. Following her heart and not her head would probably be her eventual downfall, but she found herself unable to stop her concern about a dark, soulful man and his damaged but lovely daughter.

Phoebe stared sightlessly into the closet where she'd hung her clothes only the night before. The barn-raising wasn't for another three days, but in Phoebe's experience, it was never too early to plan for the appropriate outfit. The only problem was that Phoebe had absolutely no idea what one wore to such an event.

It was presumably casual, given that they would actually be constructing a building, but casual to Phoebe and casual to the townspeople of Serendipity was probably on the far opposite ends of the fashion spectrum. And even if it wasn't, Phoebe's wardrobe was lax in anyone's definition of the word.

Up until this point, her career had been her whole life, and with that came the clothes appropriate for her celebrated status. She didn't particularly like dressing up, it was just something she did for work and didn't really give much thought to.

Now she was thinking about it.

She considered asking Chance for advice but quickly nixed that idea. Chance was a rugged, completely masculine, thoroughly country man from the top of his cowboy hat to the tips of his scuffed, dusty boots. Not exactly the kind of guy who would know anything at all about fashion. He probably couldn't tell her what kind of clothes people—women in particular—wore to barn-raising events if she'd decided to ask him.

Lucy, on the other hand—now there was an idea.

Phoebe folded two pairs of jeans over one arm and selected three different colors and styles of shirts from the closet—a rich chocolate-brown cable-knit sweater, a lavender rayon blouse and an emerald-green western shirt she'd purchased on impulse before she'd arrived in Serendipity and had yet to try on, much less wear.

She found Lucy in the living room, seated on the couch watching a comedy on TV. Since the girl's back was turned from where Phoebe had entered, she called out to her.

"Lucy, can I get your opinion on something real quick? I need a female's point of view."

To Phoebe's surprise—or maybe not so much, all

things being what they were—Lucy didn't acknowledge her at all, not even to make a rude retort.

She tried again. "I could really use your help."

She might as well not have spoken, for as much of
a response the girl gave her—which was nothing.

Maybe if she told Lucy what she wanted, the girl
would be more interested. One more time, then. "I
can't decide which pair of jeans I should wear this
weekend. I've never been to a barn-raising before."

"She can't hear you." Chance's low, rough-voiced
explanation came from behind her.

Phoebe's heart skipped a beat and then made up
for it by racing into a full gallop. It appeared the man
made it a habit of sneaking up on people. Or was it
just her he liked to freak out?

"You startled me," she accused, shaking a finger
at him. "Again."

His expression, one flash short of a scowl, didn't
change. "I thought you said you wanted help with
Lucy."

She nodded. "I do, but—"

"Then you ought to know you're speaking to dead
air space," he explained briskly, cutting her off.

"I know she's watching television, but the volume
isn't up that loud." Phoebe was uncomfortable talking about Lucy as if she wasn't there, since she
was present and only a mere two feet from where
they were standing. If she was listening to any of
this conversation…

Chance's crooked grin appeared. His smile was the only imperfect feature on his otherwise flawlessly chiseled face. Curiously enough, it was also what Phoebe found most attractive about him. It gave him character.

When he smiled—which wasn't often.

"Observe," he said, stepping forward until he was just behind Lucy. He bent down slyly, reached on either side of the girl's head, and deftly plucked a tiny pair of ear buds from her ears.

"Hey," Lucy protested, leaning back to glare at her father. "I was listening to that."

Chance just chuckled and pointed to the cell phone in his daughter's hand.

"Why do you have the television on when you have music blaring in your ears and all your attention is on texting your friends on your cell phone?"

"I'm watching the show," Lucy insisted.

Phoebe grinned. "A multitasker, like your father."

Lucy's low-browed gaze met Phoebe's. "Whatever."

"It's a private joke," Chance explained; not, Phoebe thought, that Lucy cared one way or the other.

Lucy's gaze never faltered from Phoebe's. "Like I said—whatever."

"Do you have to do this all the time?" Chance asked, clearly exasperated.

"No, it's okay," Phoebe said, stepping between father and daughter both literally and figuratively. "I don't want to bother you, Lucy. I was just wondering if you could help me pick out my outfit for Saturday."

She sensed the immediate shift of the girl's interest like a cleft in the ground after an earthquake. Was that a gleam of interest Phoebe had just seen sparking in Lucy's eyes?

For both their sakes, she hoped so. Not wanting to miss the opportunity, she held out the arm with the two pairs of jeans, one a dark wash, the other faded, folded over it.

"What do you think?"

Lucy eyed the clothing keenly, her lips twisting in thought just the way Chance's did.

After a moment, Lucy pointed at the faded denim. Phoebe probably would have nixed the darker designer jeans on her own, but she was glad for Lucy's opinion.

"And for a top?" Phoebe held up one hanger at a time for Lucy to inspect.

"This one," Lucy said, pointing to the western shirt. "It'll bring out all the different colors in your eyes. And bring the sweater for later on when it gets cold. Do you own a hat?"

"A cowboy hat?"

Lucy shrugged noncommittally. "Cowboy hat. Stocking cap. Whatever."

"I have a hand-knit beret. Personally, I think I'd look ridiculous in a cowboy hat."

Lucy shrugged again. "Probably."

Phoebe's comment had been meant as a joke, so she felt no offense that Lucy had taken it as one.

She had to admit she was surprised—and impressed—not only by Lucy's fashion sense, but by her common sense. The girl was actually being friendly, at least a little bit. Maybe there was hope after all.

Chance didn't look so convinced. "You didn't pack a T-shirt?" He swept a glance over her, his lips twisting, presumably at her city-bred idea of casual wear—nice slacks and a sweater.

Phoebe's breath caught in her throat at his open perusal, but she stood her ground. She was so *not* the T-shirt type. Even her pajamas were made of silk.

"Not one," she confirmed.

His eyebrow rose, but that was the only change in his expression.

"Guess that'll have to do, then." He turned and walked out of the room without a further word.

"You don't need a T-shirt," Lucy whispered as soon as Chance was out of hearing range. "He doesn't know anything. He's just a man."

Chance was a *man*, all right. No disagreement, there. That was part of the problem.

Maybe she would buy a T-shirt if she happened to visit one of the larger towns in the area, but she would only be giving in to country living and common sense and *not* because Chance had suggested it.

She didn't care what Chance thought about her wardrobe, or how she looked. She didn't. Really.

STATUS UPDATE: PHOEBE YATES: Baking, baking, baking!

JOSEPHINE HAWKINS MURPHY: Hooray!

Chance smothered a yawn and paused as he reached for the back door of the café. As was his custom, he'd arrived promptly at 7:00 a.m., though this morning he had been more inclined to turn off his alarm, roll over and go back to sleep. He was usually a morning person, but now he found himself as exhausted as he'd ever been in his life.

He was having trouble sleeping, and it was all because of a certain hazel-eyed woman who'd entered his life with a gale-wind tempest that blew his hard-earned tranquility away.

Chance tried not to care, which might work to a casual observer, but he couldn't lie to himself. He couldn't just go on with his life like nothing untoward was occurring.

He couldn't just ignore Phoebe, as much as he might want to.

And he *did* want to.

He sighed and turned the knob. This was going to be a hectic morning. Aunt Jo was running late and he'd have to take the first few orders himself, or else have Phoebe do it.

He suspected he'd find Phoebe busy baking cakes or pies or something. She'd left the house before he was even awake. But he had no way of preparing himself for what he encountered upon entering *his kitchen*.

White flour.

Everywhere.

The counters were covered with the powdery snowlike substance, and as for the floor—well, it wouldn't be exaggerating to say there wasn't a single spot in which he could walk that would not retain the imprint of his boot.

His jaw dropped and his eyes widened in disbelief. His mouth tried to form words, but there was nothing.

"I…you…" he stammered, but got no further.

Phoebe, who was industriously rolling out dough for pie shells, looked up at him and grinned. "Oh, my. I must have lost track of time."

Chance lifted an eyebrow. "Apparently."

"I was going to clean up this—" she paused and gestured toward the floor "—mess before you got here."

"And how much time, exactly, did you think you would need to clean up this *mess?*" he asked, exaggerating the word.

Disaster, was more like it. And he thought *he* was

untidy when he got especially creative. She definitely won the award in that department.

She shrugged, her smile wavering. "I don't know. A few minutes, I guess."

"Seriously?" His other eyebrow rose to meet the first. The woman was certifiable if she thought it would take less than half an hour to put things to right.

Only then did she really look around, and he could tell the very moment she recognized the true state of *his* kitchen, for her gaze widened considerably and the smile dropped from her lips altogether.

"I'm so sorry," she apologized immediately. "I was caught up in my baking and I thought it would be okay for me to use all the counters until you came in."

He almost chuckled.

Almost.

"I'm here now." Nothing like stating the obvious.

"And I'm getting the broom from…where is the broom located, exactly?"

He pointed to the far corner where a small industrial cart was kept, including a mop and a broom.

Sighing, Phoebe brushed the back of her hand across her cheek, leaving a thin layer of flour in its wake. Chance jammed his hands into his pockets to keep himself from acting on the nearly irresistible urge to wipe the flour away with the pad of his thumb. That kind of action, he knew, would be a mistake of monumental proportions on any number of levels.

"You're making pies?" he asked in an effort to channel his thoughts away from how attractive he found the beautifully chaotic woman.

"I'm planning to do a few pies today and maybe a chocolate cake or some brownies. I've already made a few dozen cookies. I'm sticking with the tried-and-true until I see how the townsfolk feel about my baking endeavors."

She laughed and scrunched up her face. She almost sounded nervous, though why that would be, he couldn't imagine. She'd baked in world-renowned restaurants and she was afraid of a few country critics here in Serendipity? Not likely.

"Chocolate chip?" he guessed—or rather, hoped. He hadn't had a decent homemade chocolate chip cookie in ages. His mouth watered just thinking about it.

"Uh-huh," she said, running the broom across the floor and creating a cloud of white dust in the process. "And some plain old sugar cookies. Everything's in the pastry case if you want to go see for yourself."

His throat spasmed and he shook his head. He wasn't ready to see a full pastry case—not yet, anyway. He wasn't even sure he wanted to hear how the good folks of Serendipity felt about Phoebe's baking, which he was certain they would love.

Somehow admitting that Phoebe was here and that people would appreciate her cooking seemed almost like he was betraying the memory of Lindsay. How could he wish Phoebe the best when her *best* might be better than Lindsay's ever was?

His expression must have revealed some of what he was thinking, because Phoebe was at his elbow in an instant, a worried frown on her face.

"What's wrong?" she asked softly. "You look a little pale."

He scoffed and shook his head. "The only thing that's wrong with me is that I can't find a single inch of work space in here."

He sounded gruff and he knew it, but he couldn't find it within himself to apologize.

"You don't want to try one of my cookies, then?" She sounded genuinely hurt, but the corners of her lips were turned down in what he thought might be a playful pout, so he wasn't certain. He wasn't sure about anything where Phoebe Yates was concerned.

"Maybe later." He picked up a dishrag just as the bell over the front door rang. "We have customers."

Phoebe nodded and went back to sweeping while Chance scrubbed furiously at the white-coated surfaces of the counters. His wet dishrag quickly hardened under his touch, leaving sticky clumps on the flat surfaces of the counters.

"I don't believe it," he said with a groan.

"What now?" Phoebe stopped sweeping and leaned on her broom handle.

Chance held up the sticky dishrag. "I've just created papier-mâché."

Their eyes met and she covered her mouth with her palm as she began to snicker. He held her gaze. This was not funny. It wasn't.

Yes, it was.

His lips twitched as he gave in to the low, throaty chuckle that wouldn't be denied. Papier-mâché, indeed.

"We could make a piñata," she suggested, balling up a pile of flour from the counter. Her eyes gleamed as she flicked some at him. "Or we could have a snowball fight."

He scowled. "Don't even think about it."

She shrugged, her pixielike expression hinting at mischief. "It might be fun."

"No way. I'm here to work, not to have fun." He rinsed the rag and continued scrubbing the counter.

"Well, that sounds just awful. Can't you do both? I know I can."

He narrowed his gaze on her. "Why does that not surprise me? Now get busy or neither one of us is going to get our work done today."

She tilted her head and propped one hand on the top of the broom and the other on her hip. "I'll make you a deal."

"Humph." It would be infinitely easier if he wasn't

dealing with her at all. This was his kitchen, his domain, and she was only here by his good graces. Or more to the point, because he didn't know how to say no to his Aunt Jo.

"I'll clean up the whole place and you can concentrate on getting your breakfast orders out."

Finally, a reasonable statement from an entirely irrational female.

"If…" she continued.

He groaned and tossed the dishrag into the sink. He should have known there would be a condition. There was always a condition.

"If?" he prompted, crossing his arms and doing his best to glare at her.

"*If* you taste one of my cookies."

He didn't know what he'd expected her to say, but that was definitely not it. "Are you serious?"

"Deadly. Or rather, hopefully, not *deadly*. I would really like to have your opinion on my cookies before anyone else asks for one. It's been a long time since I've done such basic work. Maybe I've lost my touch." She chuckled.

"You have spent your entire career making fancy French pastries and you're worried about your cookies?"

He was teasing her, but there was something about her expression that appeared earnest, just the hint of vulnerability in her eyes. The inherent male in him wanted to act on that hidden fragility, to protect and shelter her from whatever was bothering her. Only that was entirely unnecessary. She was psyching herself out for no reason.

"All right. I'll eat one of your cookies."

He was giving in to her demands and he knew it. It was a giant step backward, but really, how could he say no?

She bolted from the room with almost contagious enthusiasm. He vowed then and there that despite his reticence to accept her into his kitchen and his life, he would compliment her on her baking. It went entirely against the grain for him to do so, knowing he would be creating more problems than he was solving, but he just couldn't stand to be the one to burst her bubble.

"Quick, quick," Phoebe said as she dashed back into the kitchen with a tissue-wrapped cookie in her hand. She held it toward his mouth almost as if she were going to feed him.

"What's the rush?" he asked, taking the cookie from her and unwrapping it. It smelled amazing and he inhaled deeply, his mouth started to water.

"The gentlemen who work at the hardware store each asked for one," she explained breathlessly.

"Before breakfast? That's a little unusual."

"I guess it's been a while since they've seen baked goods in the pastry case. Now do me a favor and taste the thing, will you?"

Chance grinned, held the cookie to his lips, and then paused.

Phoebe shook her hands at him impatiently. It was amusing to watch her squirm.

Finally, when he thought she could stand it no longer, he took a big bite of the cookie.

Chapter Seven

STATUS UPDATE: PHOEBE YATES: I'm anxious to see how the customers at Cup O' Jo feel about my cookies.

JOSEPHINE HAWKINS MURPHY: They'll love them, of course.

Phoebe had forgotten to take a breath and her vision was beginning to fade as she watched Chance slowly, methodically chew and swallow the crisp-on-the-outside, chewy-on-the-inside chocolate chip cookie. He wasn't in any hurry to tell her what he thought, that was for sure.

He was purposefully torturing her. Why she had expected him to be a normal human being and kindly reassure her all was well with her little baking endeavor was beyond her. Chance was the least helpful man she'd ever had the displeasure of knowing.

And why did it matter, anyway? She'd never once doubted her cooking ability in the past, and these cookies were made with the simplest of recipes. Then again, she'd never cared quite so much what her customers thought.

The people of Serendipity were used to robust country cooking, which was a complete novelty to Phoebe. She thought she might be on a pretty tight learning curve trying to please the general public here. Somehow she inherently knew they wouldn't go for the kinds of things she usually baked, and it had her worried, however irrational it was.

It didn't help that Chance continued to tease her— or taunt her, more accurately.

"So?" she asked, letting her annoyance sound in her voice.

He shrugged. "So," he repeated, as if he didn't know what she was asking.

"Chance Hawkins, you'd better tell me what you think of my cookie or that will be the last one you ever taste." She swiped for the half of the cookie still left in his hand, but he quickly pulled it out of reach, dangling it over her head.

"Oh, you're scaring me," he teased with a wink.

Phoebe backed away and picked up the broom she'd set aside earlier. "Fine. Don't say anything."

She began sweeping furiously, not caring that she was making more of a mess than she was cleaning up.

"It's…" He paused thoughtfully. "Good."

Phoebe swung on him. "Good? That's all you can say about it? It's *good?* I thought you'd have more of an opinion than that."

He grinned. "I'm not your most severe critic here in Serendipity, but honestly, I have to tell you, the folks of Serendipity are going to love having you here. This cookie is awesome."

His lips twisted sardonically as he said it, and Phoebe wondered why. It was almost as if he were complimenting her despite himself.

Maybe he was. It was her fault for asking. *Awesome* wasn't quite the word she would have liked to describe her baking, but she supposed it would have to do.

"I'll go get the men their cookies, then," she said, setting the broom aside once again.

"And then you'll be back to clean my kitchen? You promised," he reminded her.

"How could I forget?" she muttered under her breath but loud enough for Chance to hear her.

She was shaking as she served the three old men their cookies. She had given them each two, one chocolate chip and one sugar, and told them the baked goods were on the house today. She held her breath as she waited for one of them to take a bite.

Like everything else the men did, they each took a bite simultaneously, and their reactions were similarly synchronized.

"Wow," said one.

"Mmm," said another.

"Fantastic," exclaimed the third, drawing out the word. "Best cookie I ever tasted."

Phoebe chuckled. "Thank you," she said simply.

"No," said the first man. "Thank *you*."

Smiling at her apparent success, she quickly took their breakfast orders, which she suspected Chance was already working on, and hurried away, though she continued to keep half an ear tuned into the way they were carrying on about her baking.

It made her feel good that she had been able to make her customers smile. She wasn't used to getting such direct feedback on her work. The food critic's column in the newspaper wasn't even remotely as satisfying as this was.

She suspected that half the town would know how the men felt about her baking within the hour. Before she could even leave the dining area, four other customers asked to try her cookies, even though it was still so early in the day.

As she expected, she found Chance already at the grill when she returned to the kitchen with a pile of breakfast orders. His back was turned to her and he didn't acknowledge her return, so she went to the sink and filled a bucket with hot, soapy water to wash the counters down without the damp flour sticking to the washrag.

Within fifteen minutes, every counter except the

one stacked with pie crusts was sparkling clean. The floor had been swept and mopped, and the cleaning items returned to the service cart.

"Well?" she asked when Chance returned from taking a few plates out to customers. "Good enough for you?"

He scratched his chin. "Wow. That was fast."

"I may be messy, but I am efficient. Now can I get back to the pies I was baking?"

"Yeah. Sure thing." He turned back to the grill and threw on some more strips of sizzling bacon.

Phoebe returned to cutting pie shells out of her dough but found the joy she usually felt in baking strangely absent. She'd been having so much fun earlier that she'd lost track of time. Now each moment seemed to drag. Her arms felt heavy and her neck was tight with strain.

Chance's presence had done more than just disrupt her day. It had killed any hope she had of getting any real baking done. Even when he didn't say a word, his presence in the room was overpowering. She'd worked with plenty of men over the years, but none so overtly rugged and masculine as Chance. She found herself watching him when his back was turned, admiring his strong build and easy movements as he cooked.

Keep your mind on your baking, she admonished herself silently. This was never going to work if she couldn't keep the pastry case full because her mind kept wandering.

She'd only just forced her mind back on her work when suddenly Chance was behind her, one hand braced on the counter beside her while he reached over her head to grab a pan hanging on a hook from the ceiling.

Excuse me would have been nice. Or he could have simply asked her to get the pan for him. But no, he had to go and exert his presence by hovering over her.

He was probably trying to intimidate her, she decided. Well, it wasn't going to work.

She attacked her pie-making with a new vengeance, placing rounds of dough into pie pans, filling them with fresh fruit and covering them with yet another round of dough. With the ease borne of years of practice, she used her fingers to pinch the dough together into a pretty pattern. She used a sharp knife to slice thin ridges in the middle of the dough in a spiral pattern.

Balancing two pie plates on one arm, she used the other to reach for the oven, which she'd preheated earlier. She was about to open the oven door when Chance laid his large hand over hers, stopping her from moving.

"Uh-uh," he said in that low, raspy voice of his.

"What?"

"You can't use the oven."

"Is that right?" She wasn't annoyed, she was angry. "Then how do you expect me to bake the pies? Put them out in the sun?"

He chuckled, but Phoebe found no amusement in the situation.

"What I mean is, you can't use the oven *now.* I have to warm up some rolls first."

She sighed. She wanted to argue, but what was the point? Chance was cooking the meals and she was just baking desserts that the café hadn't had in a while anyway, so whatever he needed to do took precedence over her baking her pies.

But still. Couldn't he have put his rolls in five minutes earlier? Why did she feel he had waited until she was ready to use the oven to suddenly decide to make rolls?

She couldn't prove that theory, however, so she backed away and placed the pies on the nearest counter.

"Those can't go there," Chance insisted. "I need that counter space to work on."

"Of course you do," she muttered.

"I'm sorry, what was that? Were you saying something about the way I work in my kitchen?"

Phoebe moved her pies back to her counter and then turned, crossing her arms in front of her as she glared at Chance's back.

"This isn't going to work, is it?" she asked pointedly.

"I don't know," he answered. "You tell me."

"Honestly, I think this kitchen is too small for the both of us. If you aren't willing to concede just a little, I might as well leave now."

Chance put his spatula down and wiped his hands on his apron. He studied her for a moment without speaking and then gave a clipped nod.

"I get what you're saying," he admitted.

"And?"

"I'll try harder. Is that what you want to hear?"

The words were right, but the attitude wasn't. It was like talking to a teenager who said one thing and meant something entirely different.

Still, it was probably the best she was going to get out of him, and he hadn't bulldozed her right out of the kitchen for having the nerve to confront him.

"You'll share oven time?"

He frowned. "I guess."

"And counter space."

"Hey, now, I told you that—"

"You need a lot of room to work," she finished for him. "We've been through all this. Now that we've had some time to work together, I think we've clearly established that we are going to be bumping into each other on a regular basis, and that we are going to have to share our toys. But I'm willing to try if you are. Agreed?"

Chance turned back to the grill and picked up his spatula. The sizzle of the bacon as he turned it over almost covered up his soft, gruff answer, but Phoebe heard it. Barely.

"Agreed."

STATUS UPDATE: PHOEBE YATES: Pies and cookies and cakes, oh, my! I'm having a wonderful time baking for the country potluck. It's a different experience altogether, and I'm loving every second of it. Or at least, almost every second. There's this man…

JOSEPHINE HAWKINS MURPHY: No wonder your pies and cookies are world-famous. You are truly blessed by God with special creativity, and I am blessed by God to get to sample it!

PHOEBE YATES: Thanks for not commenting on the man, lol.

JOSEPHINE HAWKINS MURPHY: I would never think to intrude, my dear. At least not yet.<g>

Chance sat at the kitchen table, a mug of steaming black coffee in his hands. He was waiting on the ladies to finish their personal preparations for the barn-raising, and it was taking *forever*. What, he wondered, could they possibly be doing that would take them that long? Even Lucy had not yet wandered into the kitchen, and it wasn't like the girl had to apply makeup.

She'd better *not* be applying makeup.

He sighed, thinking back over the past few days. Sharing his kitchen with Phoebe was tough on many levels. It was every bit as much of a pain as he had imagined it would be, and then some, in ways he hadn't even considered before she'd walked into his kitchen and his life.

Elbow-to-elbow, they bumped into each other all the time, which was thoroughly annoying. Sometimes Phoebe wanted to use the oven when *he* wanted to use the oven; and though she asked nicely, it still irritated him to have to share.

As if that wasn't bad enough, she lingered around every day after he closed up shop, her car keys held prominently in one hand. He knew what she was doing, even if she never said so aloud.

He didn't say anything, either. Every day, he just turned and walked away.

And every day as she passed by him in her rental car, she would slow down and gawk at him as if he were an anomaly, some strange creature walking down the side of the road.

What? Hadn't the woman ever heard of the benefits of fresh air and exercise?

If he were being honest, though, it wasn't the counter space or the ovens or even the way she stared at him like he was riding a circus elephant home from the café that bothered him most.

It was the *close proximity* thing.

He tried not to notice Phoebe as a woman, he really did; but how could he not notice her when she would become completely absorbed in her baking and would accidentally smear flour across her cheeks and dot her nose? Did she not realize how cute she looked when she did that?

And if that wasn't bad enough, she smelled delicious—some kind of vanilla-scented musk that was completely at odds with the usual smell of greasy country cooking. How was a man supposed to concentrate on his work when he was enveloped in the sweet vanilla scent of the finest French pastries—not from the pies and cookies she was baking, but exuding from the woman herself?

How fair was that? Thank goodness they'd closed the café today in honor of the barn-raising. At least there he could keep his distance from the distracting woman.

As if on cue, Phoebe entered the Hawkinses' country kitchen, rosy-cheeked and freshly showered, her eyes brimming with delight and exhilaration over the day to come. Her vanilla scent wafted in with her, and Chance inhaled deeply despite himself.

"You ready?" he asked, though it was obvious that she was clearly anticipating the day.

"I'm so excited I may burst. Do you think I'll meet everyone in Serendipity today?"

He chuckled at her enthusiasm. "You've already met practically half the town."

"You'll have to forgive me," she gushed. "It's just that this is just so completely out of my range of experience."

But not out of her comfort zone, Chance mused. He had no doubt that she would mesh right in with the locals, and apparently, she didn't, either. Everyone who'd met her at the café already like her.

What was there not to like?

Aunt Jo bustled into the kitchen. "Chance, dear, the picnic baskets are ready to be placed into the pickup. Phoebe and I will have the cooler loaded with soda and water in short order."

Chance nodded and reached for the baskets on the counter, one in each hand. They were surprisingly heavy, but then, his Aunt Jo never did anything halfway. If she was going to bring food to the barn-raising, she was going to bring *food*, and lots of it. Not only that, but Phoebe had spent the previous day baking fresh pies and cookies for the event.

Apple pies, cherry pies and rhubarb pies. Dozens of chocolate chip cookies, peanut butter cookies, and his own personal favorite, snickerdoodles. His mouth watered just thinking about it.

It didn't take long to get everything situated in the back of the truck, and Chance was antsy to get moving. It was several miles' walk to the Sparkses' ranch. If he didn't get started soon, he wouldn't be arriving until the barn was already built and the sun was setting in the western end of the sky.

Aunt Jo hopped behind the wheel, and Chance opened up the passenger door for Lucy and Phoebe. Lucy crawled in first and reluctantly scooted to the middle, effectively ignoring all the adults present with the use of her ever-present MP3 player.

Phoebe hesitated at the door.

"I don't think there's room enough for the four of us to sit," she observed. "I am happy to follow you all in my own vehicle, as long as you promise not to lose me." She chuckled at her own joke.

"Oh, no, dear. Chance doesn't ride," Aunt Jo explained before Chance could say a word.

Phoebe turned to him and addressed him directly. "I know you walk to and from work, but I was given to understand that this homestead is several miles out of town."

Chance confirmed her statement with a clipped nod.

Her unwavering hazel-eyed gaze caught his. She was quiet for a moment, her full lips pressed together. Her thoughtful perusal made him uncomfortable. He felt like she was trying to probe his mind for something, and it took all his willpower not to break the connection.

"I see," she said at last, though he hadn't of-fered her a word of explanation. "In that case, I'll walk, too."

"What a delightful idea," Aunt Jo stated enthusi-astically.

Chance thought it was a horrible idea, but he was apparently the only one not warming to the idea.

Despite theoretically being unable to hear their conversation with her music on, Lucy quickly slid over to claim the passenger seat for herself and was already reaching for the door handle.

Chance held the door handle tight, refusing to give in. It wasn't necessarily that he minded Phoe-be's company, but why should she suffer walking for several miles just because he had peculiar hang-ups? She ought to catch a ride with Aunt Jo and Lucy.

He was long past obsessing every time one of his loved ones rode in an automobile—it would have driven him crazy within a year if he had. It was only his own self he didn't trust. No matter how irrational it was—and he knew it was—he just couldn't—*couldn't*—get into a car.

Which now left the issue of Phoebe joining him on the walk to the Sparkses' house, though whether it was out of the goodness of her heart or else to try to prove her point, he didn't know.

"I don't think it's a good idea," he stated, voicing his opinion at last, though he suspected he might as well be speaking another language, for all the good it would do him. He was outnumbered, and he knew it. And by females.

"Nonsense," Aunt Jo replied. "We'll see you two at the Sparkses'."

"I'm walking. Don't try to talk me out of it," Phoebe said, a determined look on her face.

As if he could. "Suit yourself."

"Buckle up," he ordered Lucy before he closed the passenger door and waved them on their way.

Chance turned toward the road. "You didn't have to do this."

"Oh, I think I did," she replied cryptically.

What did that mean? What did she think she'd be proving by walking with him?

That she was in good shape? Any man with eyeballs in his head could see that.

That she had a kind heart? She had already demonstrated that in any number of ways, not only to him, but with Lucy and Aunt Jo.

That she cared about him? He didn't *even* want to go there.

They walked together in silence, but it wasn't uncomfortable. Thankfully, Phoebe wasn't the type of woman who felt the need to mindlessly chatter every time there was a lull in the conversation. She was a thoughtful woman in more ways than one.

To his surprise, he was the one who opened up the conversation.

"Did you really come to Serendipity just to work at Cup O' Jo?"

"Mostly," she answered in a soft, pensive tone. "It may be hard for you to fathom, but I missed the simple pleasure of baking. My world has gotten pretty hectic over the past few years."

He could well imagine. And he could understand her need for a sabbatical. But it was her first statement he remarked upon. "Mostly?"

"Well, to be honest, there was a man involved," she said with a nervous chuckle. "Isn't there always?"

Why did a knot form in the pit of his stomach at her admission? He adjusted his bandana around his throat, which felt suddenly tight.

Of course there was a man. She probably had many admirers, were he to guess.

He scowled. It was the truth, but he didn't have to like it.

"I see," he said when nothing else came to mind. He was still thinking about all of the rich, exotic men she must have met on her travels.

"Josh and I had been together for a year. When we broke up, I just wanted someplace else to go for a while, somewhere where I could find a little peace and regain my spiritual equilibrium."

"What an idiot."

"What?" She came to a grinding halt, creating a cloud of dust as she turned. "Why am I an idiot?"

He laid a consoling hand on her arm. He hadn't

even realized he'd voiced his thoughts aloud, and now she'd completely misread them.

"This Josh guy," he elaborated. "*He* is the idiot. Not you."

"Because…?"

"What man in his right mind would break up with you?" He knew his voice was getting heated, but he couldn't seem to stop himself. And he was well aware he was admitting more than he cared to.

"No. You've got it all wrong," she insisted. "Josh didn't break up with me. I was the one who ended our relationship."

"That's better, then." He released the breath he'd been holding on a sigh of relief. It wasn't like him to get riled up about anything, much less something that was clearly none of his business.

"I'm sure Josh doesn't think so. We had a good relationship. I kept thinking he might be the one, but after a year, I still wasn't sure in my heart, no matter how hard I prayed about it.

"If I'm not one hundred percent sure of myself and of him, he's not it, right? Prince Charming. The one I want to spend the rest of my life with."

"I don't believe in fairy tales," Chance remarked gruffly. He had, at one time, thought the world was full of gallant knights and lovely maidens. But not now. He'd once been married to what he'd considered the love of his life, and look how that had worked out for him.

Phoebe sighed and gestured for them to continue down the road.

"Me, either. It would be nice though, wouldn't it? Growing old together, sitting on the front porch swing watching your great-grandchildren playing in the yard?"

Chance winced. "I guess."

"Oh, Chance." Phoebe stopped so abruptly that he walked right into her. Instinctively, he grasped her around the waist so they didn't both topple to the ground.

"I'm so sorry. I wasn't even thinking about your loss. I just—I didn't think. Sometimes my mouth goes faster than my brain."

"It's all right," he said, his voice especially hoarse with emotion.

And it *was* all right, he realized as he reluctantly turned Phoebe loose. He didn't know how it had happened, but when he spoke about Lindsay to Phoebe, he experienced as much joy at the memories as he did grief. Something about Phoebe's caring nature enveloped him and spared him the hot, spiking darts of pain that he'd learned to live with for so long.

"So this isn't a permanent move, then?" he queried, wondering why it mattered to him either way.

"Didn't your aunt tell you?" she asked, surprised.

He shook his head. "Aunt Jo doesn't tell me anything. I didn't even know you were arriving in town, much less that we'd be working together, until you walked into my kitchen."

"Yeah, I got that," she mused, her voice fueled with humor. "But in answer to your question, I'm on a six-week sabbatical. In early July I'm due to start as head pastry chef at Monahan's—a new, upscale restaurant opening in Times Square. I'm quite excited. I've been working for years for an opportunity like this."

"Hmm," he answered, mulling over the fact.

They walked the rest of the way to the Sparkses' house without speaking but in companionable silence, both of them lost in their own thoughts.

"I think I see Lucy," Phoebe said, pointing to a group of young people crowding around one of the long, rectangular tables that had been set up north of the barn.

Chance looked to where Phoebe was pointing. Lucy was there, all right, slouched next to a *boy*. They appeared deep in conversation, their foreheads nearly touching.

His protective, fatherly instinct ignited and flared in his chest.

His little girl.

"What is she *doing?*"

Phoebe reached for Chance's arm, restraining him from darting forward.

"They're just sharing music," she explained in a quiet, calm tone of voice. "See? She and Brian each have one earphone. You can see the cord draped between them."

"Brian?"

"It's just a guess." Phoebe's cheeks turned an attractive rose color and she looked like she was just about to burst into delighted laughter.

This was *not* funny.

"How do you know about this Brian character and I don't?"

Phoebe gave him a mysterious smile. "Let's just say I saw it written in…the sand."

Chapter Eight

STATUS UPDATE: PHOEBE YATES: The single women of Serendipity certainly can't get enough of the chef I work with. Yet he just can't see it. Maybe he simply doesn't want to.

JOSEPHINE HAWKINS MURPHY: He's always been that way, dear. He doesn't know or care what the ladies think of him—and they do think of him!

Phoebe was having a lovely time. She knew she was a liability when it came to her lack of even the most basic knowledge of carpentry, but Chance had gallantly allowed her to hold the boards for him while he was sawing and hammering.

Wisely, for her sake, he kept all the power tools and sharp objects away from her. Kindly, also for her sake, he made it at least *look* like she was helping. But it wasn't easy.

As self-conscious as she was feeling, she was grateful when Jo appeared at her side.

"You look like you could use a break," the older woman commented sagely.

"That bad, huh?"

"No, not really."

That was a fib if Phoebe had ever heard one, especially given the collective chuckling of the women around her. She joined in their laughter.

"We're starting to set up the tables for lunch. Would you like to help?"

"Of course." Phoebe breathed a sigh of relief. Preparing and serving food was way more into her comfort zone than wielding a hammer, or even being in the vicinity of someone who was—by millions of miles, at least.

"Need some help, ladies?" An older gentleman, using a cane for balance, slowly approached. His body was slouched with age and his face was weathered, but the vital gleam in his eyes was that of a much younger man. And though the question had been addressed to the small gathering of women at large, Phoebe had the distinct impression he was talking to Jo in particular.

Her suspicion was confirmed when Jo was the one to answer.

"No, Frank, we do not need help. Ladies only

here. Now go bother someone else." On the outside it might have appeared that Jo was annoyed, yet underneath Phoebe thought she heard a note of affection.

"Not until I've been introduced to this pretty young lady," Frank countered, gesturing at Phoebe.

Jo sighed dramatically. "Phoebe, meet Frank Spencer. His son Drew is helping with the construction today, and Frank here is being a menace, as you can see. Frank, this is Phoebe Yates, our new pastry chef at Cup O' Jo. Stop by sometime and taste one of her goodies."

"I'd like that," Frank agreed readily. Phoebe didn't think his visit to Cup O' Jo would be simply to try one of her pastries, if the feisty smile he flashed Jo was anything to go by.

With another self-satisfied grin, Frank turned and hobbled away.

"Now, where were we?" Jo asked.

She scooped a neatly stacked pile of red-checked tablecloths into her arms and headed for the nearest table. At each one, Phoebe spread the cloth while Jo fastened it to the table with small plastic clips. A couple of Jo's friends, Gayle and Alice, followed with flower centerpieces and large pitchers of lemonade and iced tea.

"Are we saving any of the food for supper?" Phoebe asked, noting the long row of tables set end to end, on which there were dozens of plastic containers, Crock-Pots and casserole dishes. Enough to feed a small army.

Jo chuckled. "This is more of a graze-your-way-through-the-afternoon event. Pretty soon here we'll break for lunch. Everyone will fill up their plates at least once and then come back for more when they get hungry again."

"There's certainly no shortage of food," Phoebe remarked. "I think we could feed this crowd four times over."

"You'd be surprised how much some of those young men can put away—old ones, too, for that matter," Alice said with a chuckle. "Especially after they've been working so hard."

Phoebe glanced toward the barn, which had already been framed. Several men were nailing large sheets of plywood to the sides. Her gaze didn't rest until she found Chance among them, using a Skil saw to cut through sheets of plywood.

As always when she looked at Chance, her heart beat a little faster. She could not deny her attraction to the ruggedly handsome man. He was the type of guy any woman would do a double-take on.

As if he sensed her eyes upon him, he looked up and their gazes locked. Her breath caught in her throat. She was embarrassed to have been caught watching him, but she knew he wouldn't be able to see the rosy stain of her cheeks from this distance, so she smiled and waved at him as if nothing was amiss, as if she'd just happened to be looking at him at that moment.

Of course he didn't smile back. She hadn't really expected him to, had she? And yet she couldn't deny she was a little disappointed when he merely tipped his hat in her direction and went back to his work.

Sighing inwardly, she went back to hers, only now realizing she'd been standing there clutching a red-checked tablecloth to her chest while she openly gawked at Jo's nephew. Clearly the older women had been watching her. She swallowed nervously. What must they think of her?

"Chance is a bit of a distraction, wouldn't you say?" Gayle asked with a sly smile.

If Phoebe had colored when her gaze met with Chance's, it was ten times worse now. With the heat flooding her face now, she knew she must be a bright, flaming red. If she could have crawled underneath the table and found sanctuary beneath the draping of the cloth, she would have.

In the end, she decided to be honest. It wasn't like they were going to buy any other explanation, anyway.

"He is very handsome," she admitted.

"Mmm," Jo agreed. "And you're not the only one who thinks so." She nodded toward a small group of young women Phoebe guessed to be in their late twenties. They were ostensibly setting out plates and utensils. In truth, they were openly admiring

Chance, whose T-shirt was straining against the defined threads of his arm and shoulder muscles. As if that weren't enough, they were twittering like a flock of birds and giggling like schoolgirls.

Really? At their age?

"I don't even want to know," she muttered beneath her breath.

"Don't worry, my dear. They aren't competition."

Phoebe's gaze snapped to Jo's. "I'm sorry?"

"Those girls don't hold a candle to you. Besides, this is the first time in four years that Chance has attended a community function, and that is only because you are here."

"I'm sure you're mistaken," Phoebe protested. She wasn't even positive Chance wanted her in town, much less invading his home, and worse, his kitchen. For him to be pressing his own personal boundaries and issues on her account was completely out of the question.

Wasn't it?

"You're mistaken," Phoebe said again, more firmly this time.

"You think?" Jo asked with a conniving smile.

"He's here for Lucy." That was by far a better, more probable explanation.

"I'm sure that's part of it," Jo agreed amicably. "But I've known my nephew all his life, and I've prayed especially hard for him these past four years. The poor man has suffered so much. But now something has changed in him. Something good. And it started the day you arrived in town."

This conversation was making Phoebe appallingly uncomfortable—all prickly, like she was running through a briar patch.

Maybe she was. Fortunately, at that moment, the tinny sound of an old cow bell pealed through the air.

"Time to eat," Jo said, threading her arm through Phoebe's and drawing her toward the food tables, where a line was already forming.

Thank goodness. She heaved another sigh of relief. She'd been on proverbial rocky ground there for a moment, about to slip and fall right on her face. It would be good to have a moment to regain her equilibrium.

Her solace was short-lived. After filling their plates with a variety of hot and cold dishes that ranged everywhere from country-fried chicken to homemade spaghetti and meatballs, Phoebe and Jo found a spot at one of the tables. A moment later Chance arrived, balancing two plates stacked high with food and a tall glass of lemonade. He looked tired. Sweaty. And absolutely, breathtakingly gorgeous.

Her heartbeat picked up when he grunted and dropped down onto the seat next to hers. She didn't know how she was going to swallow even one bite of food with him sitting this close to her, especially after the conversation she'd just had with Jo.

"Where's Lucy?" Chance asked in his usual low, raspy tone that, at least to Phoebe, made him sound irritated.

"Eating with the other kids," Phoebe answered.

Chance grumbled something unintelligible.

The truly frightening thing was, his surliness no longer put Phoebe off. It didn't affect her perception of him. It was simply part of what made him unique, and in the most unexplainable way possible, attractive.

While, as she'd told Jo, she doubted she was having any effect on Chance, he was definitely having an effect on her. She couldn't ever remember feeling as light-headed and giddy over a man as she did at this moment, for Chance.

The next thing she knew, she'd be giggling and fawning over him like one of those young women she'd observed earlier. She didn't know what was happening to her. Maybe it was simply her conversation with Jo that had set her off down the rabbit hole to Wonderland, but she had the unnerving feeling it was more than that.

Much more.

All the more reason for her to keep her distance—if not physically, an impossibility with them living and working together, then at least emotionally. Chance was obviously still grieving his wife, despite the amount of time that had passed since Lindsay's death. He was just as unavailable as a man with a ring on his finger. She needed to put a cap on it.

And yet another reason to keep her distance—the gaggle of women now sitting two tables down from them. Earlier, they'd clearly been watching Chance and gossiping about him. Now, Phoebe wasn't so sure where their gazes were settling, despite the fact that he was sitting next to her on the bench.

"Are those ladies staring at me?" she whispered to Jo, who was sitting on the opposite side of her. Chance was busy stuffing food into his mouth at an alarming rate. Hopefully he wouldn't hear the conversation between her and his aunt, but she had to know what the deal was with those young women.

"You'd better believe it," Jo answered in a voice too loud for Phoebe's comfort. "They've just discovered why Chance has finally ventured out of his kitchen. It's pretty obvious they perceive you as a threat."

"Threat?" Phoebe squealed. "What threat?"

Jo shot her a knowing glance.

"Should I go talk to them?"

Jo chuckled. "That would take the wind out of their sails, now wouldn't it?"

Resolved, Phoebe turned to her own meal. She would speak to the women after she ate. She was here to make friends, not create rifts where none should exist.

She put a bite of homemade potato salad in her mouth and savored its tart goodness. Deli-made was just not the same as good country cooking. She'd be sad when she had to go back home, if just for the food alone.

But, she reminded herself, she had quite some time before she had to leave Serendipity. She would enjoy every moment of it while she could.

Chance leaned toward her, his hand across her shoulder as he whispered into her ear. His breath was warm on her neck, and it made her shiver. "Why don't you sit the rest of the afternoon out? Relax under one of those cottonwoods or something."

She arched an eyebrow. "Are you trying to get rid of me?"

He chuckled. "I tried that, already. Remember? Look how that worked out for me."

"True. I think you've met your match in the stubbornness department."

"All I'm saying is, this is supposed to be your vacation, isn't it? You're already working full-time at the café. Give yourself a break."

"I don't know." She was caving, and she could see from the triumphant expression on his face that he knew it. "What are your neighbors going to think if I don't do my share?"

His brow shot up. "Not do your share? So far this morning you've spent several hours of hard labor helping me prepare lumber for the barn and then you helped Aunt Jo get the tables ready for service. You deserve a break after that."

"You're not taking one," she pointed out with a stubborn tilt to her chin.

"Yes, but I'm a guy. Look around you. A lot of young women aren't rushing to get into the fray of things." He gestured to the same group of women Phoebe had been observing earlier.

"That is so—" Phoebe paused, fuming. *"Sexist!"*

He shrugged. "I'm just saying—"

"Yes, I hear what you're saying. Forget it. I'm going to help the ladies with the clean-up and then I'll be back bothering you again."

"Great," Chance groaned. "A woman under my feet. Just what I needed."

"Maybe that's exactly what you need," she challenged, propping her hands on her hips.

He shook his head. "In the words of my daughter Lucy, *whatever*." His self-deprecating grin showed Phoebe just how he meant it.

He was teasing her. It was a baby step forward in the progress of their relationship—their *working* relationship, that is—but it was a start. Phoebe prayed it would be the first of many.

STATUS UPDATE: PHOEBE YATES: Whew! A barn-raising is hard work—but it's worth it just to sample all the food. I've met so many nice people here. I'm glad I came.

JOSEPHINE HAWKINS MURPHY: I was hoping you'd start to feel that way, dear.

* * *

Chance wiped his sweaty brow against his sleeve and sighed. Having lived in Serendipity all his life, he'd grown up with numerous barn-raising type events, which were community functions as much as they were Christian charity to any neighbor who had fallen upon hard times.

He'd learned his way around a hammer and a Skil saw when he was a young teenager, and though he had always been reserved, he'd enjoyed helping out— at least until Lindsay died.

Carpentry was an art form, much like cooking, only it was a good deal more physically strenuous. Despite walking to and from work every day, he was suddenly feeling very out of shape—at least for this type of hard labor. His arms and shoulder muscles were already beginning to bunch up and get sore and tight. He didn't even want to think about how he was going to feel tomorrow.

He groaned and flexed his shoulders. Maybe, at the ripe age of thirty-two, he was getting old. The thought made him chuckle.

"What's so funny?" Phoebe asked, startling him. He hadn't even seen her approach.

"You here to help?" He asked his own question instead of answering hers.

"I am."

"About time. I thought I'd lost you to the Little

Chicks." He nodded his chin toward a small group of young women.

"Little Chicks?"

He shrugged. "That's what my friends and I called them back in high school." He paused. He could see how Phoebe might think that sounded a little condescending. It *was* a little condescending, now that he thought about it. Shrugging, he plunged on. "They were all freshmen when we were hotshot seniors. Always fawning over us. Giggling. Cheeping at each other."

He'd expected a disapproving smile, but Phoebe smothered a laugh.

"It appears some things haven't changed," she commented, pinching her lips in an effort to control her amusement. "They're still fawning. And they're still giggling. I get where you'd think that they sound like chickens, but I was leaning toward geese, myself."

"Ha!" He laughed out loud. Really laughed. And it felt good. "And so why were you hanging out with that bunch, again? I saw you talking to them after lunch."

Her shimmering hazel eyes widened and she made the funniest face, as if she'd just swallowed a whole frog or something. Then she grinned and shrugged.

"I'm just out there trying to make new friends. Those women looked to be around my age, and they obviously aren't married."

"Obviously," Chance agreed, studying her intently. The woman had no fear. She easily made friends with everybody.

Phoebe did her best to pitch in as they put the finishing touches on the barn. She didn't know a thing about carpentry, but her willing spirit went far to help. And she was a good sight better to look at than the bunch of dirty, sweat-soaked men milling around.

"It doesn't look finished," Phoebe observed when the men began putting their tools away and migrating back toward the food.

"It's not. We've done the majority of the work, but the Sparks family will still have to insulate the walls and put shingles on the roof."

Phoebe laughed. "It's a good thing they have four boys, then. Still, I imagine they saved a bundle with all the work that's been done today."

"And the neighbors had an excuse to get together, not that they need one."

"Killing two birds with one stone," she agreed.

"Shh," he said in an exaggerated whisper. He put a hand on her shoulder and bent his head close to hers with a conspiratorial air. "The Little Chicks might hear you say that. You wouldn't want to alarm them with all your talk about murdering poor, innocent birds."

She leaned back to smile at him. The movement stirred up her vanilla scent and Chance's head started to spin.

With his heart jolting into his throat, he quickly stepped away from her. He'd forgotten himself there for a moment. This wasn't what he wanted. His teasing, he realized, might be interpreted by Phoebe to be flirting.

It *was* flirting, he reluctantly admitted to himself. And he wasn't ready for that. The woman rattled him to the core, especially when she graced him with that warm, open smile of hers.

What a quandary.

What a difference a week could make.

What was he going to do?

"Are we waiting for something now?" she asked.

"More food," he answered, patting his lean stomach. He was relieved to have something neutral to talk about, because his feelings were anything but neutral. "And it's a good thing, too. I'm famished."

"You worked hard."

He nodded. "So did you."

They each served themselves, piling platefuls of food and then Chance led the way to the table farthest and most isolated from the crowd.

"You can go sit with my aunt if you'd rather," he remarked, nodding his head toward the older woman, who was merrily chatting away with her own group of friends.

"She looks like she's enjoying herself," Phoebe remarked thoughtfully. "But I'd rather sit here with you, just the same."

"Not too isolated for you?"

"No, not at all. My brain is entirely overstimulated from all the people I've met today."

Chance's brow rose. He highly doubted she was telling him the truth. Most likely, she was just trying to be nice.

She smiled mysteriously and forked a bite of a colorful pasta salad into her mouth.

"I'm looking forward to attending church tomorrow," she said when she had chewed and swallowed. "I know Serendipity is small, but I can't believe everyone in town fits into that small little chapel I saw there on Main Street. Or are there other churches I don't know about?"

Chance winced as if a lightning bolt had just zapped him from above. He hadn't been near a church in four years.

"Not everyone goes to church," he replied gruffly, clamping down his emotions. He was not going to go there.

"Oh," she murmured, sounding both hurt and surprised, though why she should feel either was beyond him.

"Surely not everyone who lives in the Big Apple drops what they are doing on Sunday morning to attend church?"

Her extraordinary hazel eyes widened. "Well, no, but—"

"Sorry." He apologized quickly, but he knew he

still sounded as surly and withdrawn as he felt. "I'm just being facetious."

"Yes, you are," she agreed.

This time *he* was surprised.

"You didn't have to agree with me," he muttered crossly.

"No?"

"I guess I should have expected that from you. You're nothing if not honest."

"I am," she agreed. "I take it you don't attend the service? I had the impression you were a churchgoing man."

He couldn't imagine where she'd gotten that notion from. "No, not really. Aunt Jo and Lucy faithfully attend every week, though, so you can go with them."

"I will, thank you." Her head was tilted to one side, and she was staring at him speculatively. He wanted to squirm under her sharp gaze, but he kept himself carefully still.

"Do you mind my asking you a question?"

"Probably."

Chance sighed inwardly. He wasn't annoyed, exactly. More like discouraged. He'd actually been enjoying the day, and his time with Phoebe; that is, until she'd gone all serious on him.

"Why did you stop going?"

How could she possibly have guessed that? He nailed her with his gaze. "Who says I ever did?"

She shrugged but her expression told him she had

no doubt she was right, and she was still waiting on his answer.

"Maybe I like sleeping in on Sundays. It's my only day off from the café."

"Maybe." She didn't sound convinced.

"Chance did go to church all the time, up until Lindsay died." The voice of Chance's former father-in-law, Lindsay's father, made him nearly jump out of his seat, except that the man had clamped an iron-hard hand down on his shoulder.

"Douglas," Chance greeted coarsely through a throat which had gone dry.

Things had gone from bad, to worse, to impossible, all in a matter of moments, like a snowball gaining momentum down a hill in an avalanche. Chance couldn't keep up.

This was *exactly* why he didn't attend community functions. It wasn't only that he didn't want to be with people in general—neighbors, some close friends, who would look at him with sadness or pity, neither of which he wanted.

Or deserved.

But this—running into Lindsay's parents, was like his worst nightmare come to life. Every muscle in his body was squeezed so tightly he thought he might implode, and in some ways, he wished he would. It would certainly be easier on him than facing Douglas and Evie Carlson.

"How are you, son?" Douglas asked gently.

"We've missed you," Lindsay's mother added.

Chance vainly adjusted the black bandana around his throat, but the choking sensation he was feeling didn't lessen. He couldn't bear to face them, afraid of the condemnation in their gazes. He didn't turn, nor did he speak.

Suddenly, under the table, Phoebe grasped his hand and gave it a light squeeze, her message clearly related.

He was not alone.

But this was his dilemma, his own personal nightmare, and it would never go away—or, apparently, get any easier. Even though Lindsay's parents appeared outwardly friendly, he could only imagine how they felt in their hearts.

Their daughter—their only child—was dead. And it was all because of him.

When Chance didn't answer, Douglas sighed and patted him on the back.

"Well, it was nice seeing you," Evie said with a false gayness to her voice that made Chance cringe so hard he wanted to fold in on himself. There was no way they were happy to see him, and he didn't blame them one bit. He was a living, walking reminder of all they had lost.

"You make sure he takes care of himself, yes?" Douglas directed his question to Phoebe.

Chance groaned and shook his head. He didn't want Phoebe involved in any part of this.

"I will, sir," Phoebe answered without hesitation. It was just like her to accept such a challenge, even though it was none of her business. She squeezed his hand again, though whether it was a gesture of comfort or of something else, he did not know.

"You didn't introduce me," she remarked quietly after the couple had left.

Chance didn't look at her, choosing instead to stare sightlessly at a point in front of him. "Lindsay's parents."

"They seemed nice." Her voice was soft and hesitant, which only served to make Chance's emotions swell inside of him.

"They are."

"I don't understand," she said, running her hand up his arm to his biceps.

"You can't know," he said, his already abrasive voice breaking.

"Know what?" It was the caring and concern in her voice that he didn't want.

Didn't need.

And in the end, it was what did him in.

He stood so quickly he knocked the folded chair out from under him. All of the emotions which had tortured him for so long—rage, guilt, grief, sorrow, love—all converged into one as he hovered over her, his shadow blocking the sun.

"I killed Lindsay," he growled through his anguish. "She's dead because of me."

Chapter Nine

STATUS UPDATE: PHOEBE YATES: Please pray for me, and for the family I'm staying with, that God will mend their hearts. I only hope I can help.

JOSEPHINE HAWKINS MURPHY: Just being here helps us, my dear. And thank you for your prayers. They are most welcome.

Phoebe couldn't get Chance   and what he'd confessed to her—out of her mind. He'd stalked off immediately after his outburst and she hadn't seen him on the Sparkses' property again. In the end, she'd ridden home with Jo and Lucy.

She spent a restless night, in turn trying to decipher what his declaration truly meant and praying for him to find peace. Even attending church didn't help. Though it was a lovely chapel and a meaningful service, she couldn't pay attention to the sermon or the songs. Her mind kept wandering back to Chance, wondering where he was and how he was feeling.

All she knew was that when he had left he was in a very dark state of mind. And that whatever else he may or may not have done in his life, he had *not* killed his wife. Anyone with half a brain could see how much he had loved her, how he grieved for her still.

No wonder he was usually so quiet and withdrawn, carrying around a burden like that.

What confused her was how Lindsay's parents had somehow set him off. What she had witnessed between them was not at all what Chance had seen and heard. Phoebe was a good judge of character. She could tell that the Carlsons were reaching out to him in kindness, and he had rejected them.

But why?

Out of some misguided sense of guilt over whatever had truly transpired the night of the car accident? Clearly Lindsay's parents didn't blame Chance for their daughter's death, so why would Chance assume they did? Why had he shut them out, when they could have all supported each other in their grief?

It didn't make sense, and Phoebe knew the only way she was going to find out the truth would be to ask Chance about it straight-out and face-to-face. The only problem with *that* strategy was that she didn't see him on Sunday—at all. If he was home, and she wasn't sure he was, he had barricaded himself in his bedroom, not even coming out to share a meal with the family.

Aunt Jo and Lucy simply went on about their lives as if this was a normal occurrence in the Hawkinses' household, for Chance to hole himself up like that.

Maybe it was.

When Chance arrived at the café Monday morning, he did not even so much as look at Phoebe, much less talk to her. He went on about his work as if she wasn't even there, except to step aside whenever they might have collided, and making sure they never touched, not even their elbows.

Over the course of the day, Phoebe went from surprised to indignant to downright angry. Chance remained as silent and broody as he ever was, leaving Phoebe wishing men in general and Chance in particular to any number of unsavory ends.

After she'd finished with her daily baking, she didn't even bother to wait for Chance to finish his own work, as she usually did. Fuming, she sped off down the road leaving a trail of dust behind her.

But any thought of what she should do about Chance went right out of her head when Lucy came flying out the front door of the house the moment Phoebe pulled up.

Something was wrong.

Very wrong.

She could see it on the girl's panicked, tear-streaked face.

"Lucy, what happened? Are you okay?" Phoebe asked as she unbuckled her seat belt and opened the car door. Her level of concern rose with every second, and she was unable to breathe around the lump in her throat.

"It's Auntie Jo," Lucy cried, new tears springing fresh to her eyes. "Oh, Phoebe, I don't know what to do!"

Alarm coursed through Phoebe. Jo hadn't been feeling well and, at Phoebe and Chance's urging, had again taken the day off to rest.

Lucy was nearing hysterics. Phoebe gently grasped her shoulders and forced the girl to look at her, all the while praying for guidance. Lucy shuddered, and Phoebe knew her own hands were shaking.

"Take a deep breath, hon," she ordered.

Lucy gulped for air.

"Now, take me to your Auntie Jo. Do you know what's wrong with her?"

She urged the girl forward, keeping a reassuring arm around her shoulders. Lucy broke into fresh tears as they entered the house.

"She's in the kitchen," Lucy said, her breath catching. "I wasn't in the room, but I think she was mopping the kitchen floor when she slipped on a puddle of water." Her voice skipped up a notch, nearly frantic with anxiety. "She can't move, and she's in a lot of pain. Maybe she broke something."

"Did you call 911?" Phoebe asked as they entered the kitchen. She tried to keep her voice calm against the pounding of her heart.

Lucy nodded and pointed to her cell phone, which was lying open on a counter next to Jo. Thankfully, the older woman was conscious, but she was obviously in a lot of pain, though she was trying not to show it.

"Good girl," she told Lucy. "Now see if they are still on the line." Phoebe knew emergency operators generally talked callers through until the ambulance arrived, and she hoped they hadn't disconnected when Lucy had dropped the phone in her haste to meet Phoebe at the door. Talking to the operator would give Lucy something useful and productive to do, rather than just stand around and worry.

Phoebe knelt by Jo and reached for her hand.

"Are you okay?" she asked gently, and then immediately shook her head. "What a stupid question. Of course you're not okay. What hurts?"

"It's this hip of mine," Jo complained, her voice shaking and her lips pinched in agony. "I guess it finally got the best of me."

"Looks like," Phoebe agreed, squeezing her hand. "We've got help on the way. Lucy, how far out is the ambulance?"

"Just a couple of minutes," Lucy answered, cupping her palm over the receiver. "I think I hear the sirens now."

"Keep the phone with you and go out front to wait for them," Phoebe directed. "I'll stay here and keep your Auntie Jo company."

"Thank you, dear," Jo said as soon as Lucy was out of earshot.

"For what?" Phoebe asked, surprised.

"For helping Lucy that way. Your calm voice and firm actions did just the trick. I was half afraid she was going to go completely hysterical on me. Thank our good Lord that you showed up when you did."

Phoebe shook her head and lowered her brow, trying to look threatening. "You put a good scare into both of us. Don't do that again. Besides, Lucy did just what she needed to do—she called 911 right away. I'm proud of her."

Despite the fact that she was clearly in agonizing pain, Jo beamed up at her. "So am I, dear. So am I."

As the ambulance and another rescue vehicle pulled up in front of the house, the sound of sirens reached Phoebe's ears.

"I think the ambulance just pulled up," she reassured the older woman. Jo closed her eyes on a sigh and gripped Phoebe's hand tightly.

"Don't you worry, dear. God and the paramedics will take care of me."

A moment later, Lucy led the first paramedic

into the kitchen. Looking to be about Phoebe's age, the EMT was shaggy-haired and unshaven, but his friendly eyes and wide smile would charm any woman between zero and eighty years of age. He was certainly having that effect on Jo, who smiled—or grimaced, at least—and reached up to pat the man's cheek as he dropped down beside her and opened his medical bag.

"Hello, Zach, dear," Jo said. "I'm sorry to drag you all the way out here on my account."

"You didn't have to hurt yourself to get me to come see you," he teased gently as he checked her pulse and her blood pressure. "Tell me where it hurts."

Jo groaned. "At the moment, everywhere. I've fallen and I can't get up. How cliché is that?"

"She has a bad hip—her left one, I think," Phoebe supplied, moving out of the way so the paramedic could work. She walked to Lucy's side and placed a comforting hand on her shoulder.

Another paramedic entered bearing a backboard, followed by two men in firemen's gear who maneuvered a gurney into the room.

The first EMT—Zach—was clearly the leader of the bunch. He directed the other men, and within minutes, they had carefully rolled her onto the backboard, lifted her to the gurney and had transported her into the back of the ambulance.

Phoebe and Lucy followed the men out. Phoebe was much more concerned than she let on. Jo was trying to make light of the situation, probably for Phoebe's sake as well as Lucy's, but her face was as white as a sheet and her fists were tightly clenched on the blanket covering her.

"It figures the one time I have four gorgeous men visit me in my home I'm down for the count," Phoebe heard her tell the EMT that had crawled into the back of the ambulance with her.

The woman had an inner strength and faith in God Phoebe could only aspire to.

She pulled Zach aside. "Jo would never complain about it, but she's clearly in a lot of pain. Can you give her something to help?"

Zach nodded reassuringly. "Unfortunately, it's an hour's drive to the nearest hospital, but we're already setting her up with an IV drip. Once that's in we'll be able to give her some pain meds to keep her comfortable."

"Can we go with her in the ambulance?" Lucy asked hesitantly.

Zach smiled at Lucy, but his eyes were on Phoebe. "I'm afraid we've only got room for one passenger."

And it couldn't be Lucy.

Zach didn't have to say the words out loud. Lucy wouldn't know what to do with herself once they got to the hospital. She would be scared and alone and maybe even in the way.

"Don't worry about it. I'll take you in my car, hon," Phoebe offered gently.

After one last pleading look at Zach, which he returned with a compassionate and reassuring smile, Lucy nodded.

"We'll be right behind them, I promise," Phoebe vowed. "But we need to go and pick up your father first, don't you think?"

By the time Phoebe had gotten directions to the hospital and waved off the ambulance, Lucy was already in the car. She didn't look any better than she had earlier, despite the fact that her great-aunt was now safe in the capable hands of the paramedics and on her way to the hospital. If anything, Lucy looked worse than ever.

"She'll be fine," Phoebe assured her as she turned the car around on the driveway. "You heard what Zach said—they'll give her some pain medication to keep her comfortable on her ride to the hospital. We'll see her soon."

"He won't come," Lucy stated miserably.

"What? Who?"

"My dad. He won't come with us."

"What do you mean he won't come with us? This is an emergency, and your aunt is family. Of course he'll come."

"No, he won't."

"Why not?"

"Have you ever seen him in a car?"

"Well, no, but—"

"He doesn't drive a car, or even ride as a passenger in one. Not ever."

Phoebe had a bad feeling about this, but she wasn't going to tell Lucy that. "Be that as it may, I'm sure he'll make an exception this time."

Lucy gave a frustrated snort and crossed her arms in a self-comforting gesture.

"No, he won't," she said again.

"Well then, we'll just have to make him listen to reason, won't we?"

"Good luck with that," Lucy muttered under her breath.

"We don't need luck, honey. We have God."

"What? Is God going to zap my dad with lightning or something?"

Lucy was making a genuine effort to lighten the mood, and Phoebe flashed her a supportive grin. "Probably not. Makes you think though, doesn't it?"

Lucy smothered a laugh.

"Seriously, though, let's pray together—for your aunt, and for your dad, too."

STATUS UPDATE: PHOEBE YATES: I have another URGENT prayer request. A dear friend fell and broke her hip. We don't know how bad the damage is yet. Please pray for her health and safety, and for her family to find peace in God.

* * *

Chance was about halfway home when Phoebe's car passed him, then slowed and turned his direction, pulling up next to him. To his surprise, Lucy was in the passenger seat.

What was up with that?

Phoebe rolled down the passenger-side window.

"Get in," she ordered in a no-nonsense tone of voice.

He shook his head, intending to ignore her demand.

"No, thank you. I'd rather walk," he said casually, and then started off down the road. He and Phoebe had already been over this ground. Why was she forcing the issue again—especially with Lucy here to see the whole thing? It wasn't like she was going to get him to change his mind—not even for his daughter.

Phoebe's car jerked forward as she pumped on the gas pedal and then skid to a stop in front of him, the hood of her car blocking his path.

"Do *not* argue with me," Phoebe said firmly, almost menacingly. "Get. In. The. Car."

Chance scowled. Why wouldn't the woman just let it be, already? "Again, no."

He had no idea what she was trying to accomplish by pulling her car in front of him. It wasn't like he couldn't walk around it, and he proceeded to do so. Let Phoebe think whatever she wanted. He was *not* getting into the car.

"Your aunt had an accident."

Phoebe's words caused him to stumble, and he pulled up abruptly, halting dead in his tracks. His heart slammed into his chest. He spun around and walked back to the car, leaning into the passenger-side window.

"What happened? Is she okay?"

"She apparently slipped on the wet kitchen floor when she was mopping. They think she broke her hip, although they won't know for sure until they get her to the hospital."

"Where are they taking her?"

"Mercy Medical Center in San Antonio. I told them we'd be right behind them. Now please, Chance. Get in the car."

Fear clutched at Chance's throat and he broke into a cold sweat. His palms were instantly clammy. His heart was pounding so hard he could hear it in his ears.

Phoebe was asking the impossible. Maybe if he'd conquered his anxiety earlier—*years* earlier—he might have been okay. But with each passing month, he had allowed his irrational fear to grow until it had become a monster he truly dared not face and conquer.

He'd always considered himself to be a strong man, but secretly, he knew the truth. He was weak. And he was terrified. He wanted to pray, but how could he turn to God now, after shunning Him for so many years? His pride simply wouldn't allow it, not even now.

"I can't," he admitted, his voice scratchier than usual because of his dry throat. Instinctively he reached for the black bandana he always wore around his neck, adjusting it over the scar.

"Yes, you can," Phoebe insisted. "Didn't you hear what I said? Your aunt is in the hospital. She needs you." She clutched the steering wheel with both fists, probably to rein in her temper.

It sounded as if she was getting annoyed with him. He supposed if he was in her place he'd be a little ticked off, as well. But that didn't change anything.

"You and Lucy go ahead to the hospital. Call me when you have an update on her condition. Tell her I love her."

"Tell her yourself." Phoebe was out of the car and up in his face so quickly he barely saw the car door open. Though she was several inches shorter than he, she was still quite formidable. She'd stepped into his personal space and was glaring up at him with so much determination it was almost steaming out of her pores.

"Look. I don't have time to argue with you, so I'm not going to try." Phoebe's voice was almost a growl. "Clearly you have some serious issues to work through, and if it were for any other reason, I'd let you do what you want and not butt into your private business."

"Glad to hear it," he mumbled.

"I'm not heartless, Chance, whatever you may think of me. But your Aunt Jo is your family. She needs your strength right now. *You* need to be there. You need to be *there*," she repeated, changing the emphasis.

"You don't understand."

"No, I don't," she agreed, her voice suddenly soft. She reached forward. Chance thought perhaps she was going to grab his shirtfront in her fist. Instead, she laid her palm over his heart.

"You're a strong man," she said, her voice dropping so only he could hear it. "More than you know. Dig into that strength. It comes from God. Wrap it around your heart. He'll help you through this."

He closed his eyes, trying to will up the power she was so certain he had within himself.

"Think about it. Jo isn't the only one who needs you right now. Lucy was the one who found your aunt. She's terrified and in shock and about to shatter into a million pieces. If you can't do it for your aunt, then at least be there for your daughter."

That was playing dirty, but Phoebe was right. Lucy did need him, and probably Aunt Jo, as well. Chance clenched his fists and forced himself to breathe.

He couldn't look Phoebe in the eyes. He was afraid she'd see what a coward he really was.

She reached up and framed his face with her hands, drawing him to look at her, regardless.

"I don't know what burden you are carrying around with you, but you need to know that God forgives you," she whispered, tears springing to her eyes. "Now you need to forgive yourself."

Unshed tears burned in his eyes, as well, but with effort, he blinked them back.

There was such compassion, such *strength* in her gaze, that he could not look away.

"You're a difficult woman, you know that?" he muttered, threading his fingers through the curls at the back of his neck.

"So I've been told." *Now get in the car* was implied but not spoken.

He nodded before he could talk himself out of it and reached for her hand. If he was going to do this, he was going to need all the support he could get.

Every muscle in his body tightened as he approached the car. The air burned in his lungs.

"Hop out, Luc," he said as he opened the passenger door. "You're going to have to sit in the backseat." He tried to smile to reassure Lucy, not to mention himself, but he wasn't so sure he succeeded in the attempt.

Lucy's already huge green eyes widened to enormous proportions and her jaw dropped open but she didn't waste any time switching to the backseat.

He dropped into the front seat and buckled up. This was it. He hoped Phoebe was ready, because there was every likelihood that he might break down into a full-fledged panic attack. He felt like an idiot. He didn't even want to know what Phoebe thought of him.

Phoebe slid behind the wheel and flashed him a re-assuring smile as she started the engine. He clenched his hands into fists on his lap as he nodded back at her.

Green light. Ready or not, this was a go.

He closed his eyes and, with Phoebe's reminder of God's presence fresh on his mind, he did something he hadn't done in years. He prayed. For himself and for his family. It was a good reminder of why he was taking this risk.

For Aunt Jo. For Lucy.

For Phoebe.

Or at least, because of her strong-armed tactics. Stubbornness and determination were her strong suits. No one else had been able to coax him near a car in four years. And then along comes this dimin-utive-sized, enormous-hearted woman and here he was, traveling by car to a hospital an hour away.

Surprisingly, the ride didn't seem as bad as he thought it might be. Now that he was settled, he was more concerned about his aunt than he was for him-self. Phoebe was a careful driver, never speeding or taking risky chances behind the wheel.

Of course, to him, every move seemed like a risky chance. But Phoebe, the kindhearted person that she was, was clearly aware of his trepidation and drove accordingly.

As they traveled, Phoebe filled him in on what had happened, how Lucy had been the one to find Aunt Jo and call 911. Phoebe's voice was full of pride at Lucy's actions and as she commended the girl for a job well done. Lucy didn't seem affected by the praise, at least not in either of the ways Chance would have thought.

She *should* be proud of the way she'd handled herself. She *could* be cutting Phoebe out again with the use of some blistering retort from her sharp tongue.

But Lucy was quiet. Too quiet. And she wasn't even listening to her music. Maybe she was still in shock. Chance prayed even harder.

"You okay?" Phoebe asked Chance as she pulled into the hospital visitor's lot and parked.

Chance nodded. "I hope Aunt Jo is faring as well as I am right now." Now that he was here, he was even more anxious to see his aunt and find out her condition.

"I'm sure she is. Let's check in at the emergency room and see if she's been admitted to the hospital yet."

It took them a few minutes to cut through the usual hospital red tape, but eventually they learned that Aunt Jo had been admitted to a ward and was now awaiting surgery on her shattered left hip. Apparently she was going to get those steel rods whether she liked them or not. Chance only wished he could have convinced her to have her surgery *before* she'd fallen and hurt herself.

But then, this was Aunt Jo. It wouldn't take any less than a major accident to get that stubborn woman to pay attention to her own needs.

The three of them were quiet as they made their way up to the fourth floor where Aunt Jo's room was located. Phoebe looked to be deep in thought and Lucy's expression was downright terrified. He couldn't imagine what the poor girl had been through, finding her aunt the way she had.

He brushed her silky hair back with his palm and then settled his hand on her shoulder. "She's gonna be all right, Luc," he whispered.

"I know." She shrugged his hand away.

At least she was acting a little bit more like her old self again, which was probably a good thing.

They reached the nurses' station on the fourth floor and Chance asked if they could see Aunt Jo.

The nurse quickly perused the three of them, and then her gaze landed back on Chance. "Are you family?"

"Yes." Chance didn't hesitate for a second. He reached for Phoebe's hand and laced his fingers through hers while simultaneously drawing Lucy close to his side. This would not be the time for either one of them to balk or try to refute his words, and they must have sensed that, for both of them played along.

Lucy was the first one in the door, followed closely by Phoebe, who might have dropped Chance's hand if he would have let her, which he didn't. He needed her support. Or at least that was what he told himself. He knew he'd eventually have to explain his actions to both Aunt Jo and Lucy, but at the moment, that was the least of his problems.

Lucy rushed to the far side of her aunt's bed and took her hand. "Auntie Jo, are you all right? I was so scared when they took you away in the ambulance."

Aunt Jo was groggy, probably from the pain medicine they'd given her, but she smiled at Lucy just the same. "I'm fine, love. I'm too tough an old bird to let something silly like a fall crack me up."

Tough didn't even begin to cover it. Chance chuckled softly.

Aunt Jo's gaze leaped from Lucy to Chance and Phoebe, and he could see the very moment she realized the two of them were still holding hands.

He froze. Aunt Jo having the accident was bad enough. He didn't want to add a heart attack to her current list of ailments.

Yet here he was, his hand comfortably intertwined with Phoebe's.

Here he was. Period.

He waited for shock or astonishment to register on Aunt Jo's face. Instead, her pale green eyes brightened and she nodded, looking entirely—what?

Satisfied? Pleased with herself?

"Thank you again for all your help, Phoebe," Aunt Jo acknowledged, her gaze turning to the woman by Chance's side. Chance wondered how she could be so cheerful after all she'd been through this day and the amount of pain she must be experiencing, but there it was.

"And Chance, dear," she continued, her pleased gaze shifting to him. "I knew you'd come."

Chapter Ten

STATUS UPDATE: PHOEBE YATES: We're waiting for my friend to go into surgery, so keep praying for all of us, and for God to guide the surgeon's hands as he works.

Count on Jo to lighten the mood, Phoebe thought. The expression on Chance's face was priceless. He looked like someone had just splashed ice-cold water in his face. Maybe it was the aftereffects of shock, but Phoebe had to bite her lip to keep from chuckling.

"H-how did you—" Chance stammered. "What do you mean you knew I'd come? I haven't—"

"Been in a car since the accident," Jo finished for him.

He jammed his fingers into the curls at the back of his neck and nodded.

"I'm glad you're here for me," Jo continued.

"Where else would I be?" Chance's already scratchy voice was especially low and rasping.

"But more than that, you stepped up for Lucy and Phoebe. I'm proud of you, dear."

Chance moved to the bedside and gently embraced his aunt. He was so tender, so careful not to hurt her that it brought a raw lump of emotion to Phoebe's throat just to watch.

He swiped a hand down his face as he stood. Phoebe wondered if the casual movement was to brush away tears. She thought maybe so. He wasn't at all the gruff, hard-hearted man that he presented to the outside world. Instead, Phoebe had found him to be a man who felt deeply and devotedly.

"What time is your surgery scheduled for?" Phoebe asked, giving Chance a moment to compose himself.

"As soon as the on-call surgeon arrives. You'll stay with me until then?"

"Of course," all three agreed immediately.

Jo was probably the strongest and most determined woman Phoebe had ever met, but even so, the older woman couldn't hide the tiny flashes of fear in her eyes. Phoebe wondered if Chance saw it as well.

She moved up next to Chance. Lucy held one of Jo's hands and Chance the other, so Phoebe gently brushed a palm over Jo's shoulder.

"We'll wait with you until they take you away for

surgery," she assured the older woman. "And we'll be here when you wake up."

"Oh, dear, that's not necessary. Who's going to run the café?"

"The café can wait," Chance said gruffly.

"I don't want to be a bother," Jo protested, though she was clearly beginning to weaken her resolve.

"Auntie Jo," Lucy protested. "You aren't a bother!"

"See?" Phoebe said, her voice forceful. "It's decided, then."

Jo looked as if she was going to argue further, but in the end she simply nodded and released a tired sigh.

"Are you in pain?" Chance asked solicitously and a little worriedly. "I can get a nurse for you."

Jo's gaze met Phoebe's and a spark of humor returned to her eyes as they shared an inside, thoroughly female joke. Count on a man to want to *do* something to fix the problem. Or at least pretend to when he really had no control at all.

But there *was* something they could do, Phoebe realized.

"Chance?"

"Hmm?" His gaze flickered to her.

"Your aunt will be going into surgery soon. Shall we pray for her?"

Phoebe knew she was taking a big risk by asking a question like that, and if Chance chose to see it that way, he could feel like she was putting him on the spot.

While she doubted he would show his resentment, she braced herself for his indifference and for him to blow off the whole idea of prayer as a waste of time. Instead, he placed his aunt's hand in Phoebe's and took her other one, silently inviting her into the family circle as he reached for Lucy's hand, as well.

Phoebe held Jo's hand and waited, wondering if Chance expected her to do the praying.

He cleared his throat. "I, uh, haven't done this for a long time, so I may be a little rusty."

Phoebe squeezed his hand and he squeezed back.

"Heavenly Father," he started softly, reverently—not at all what one would expect from a man who claimed not to believe in God. "We lift up Aunt Jo and ask You to be with her. Give her peace and comfort. Guide the surgeon's hands as he works. In Jesus' Holy Name, Amen."

He glanced at Phoebe, clearly looking for reassurance. She smiled back at him, her heart welling with emotion. His prayer had been heartfelt. Real.

Aunt Jo sniffled, and both Phoebe and Chance were instantly on the alert.

"What's wrong?" Chance asked, a note of panic to his raspy voice.

Jo smiled through her tears. "Nothing is wrong, dear. In fact, everything is so very, very right."

Chance looked bemused.

Jo's gaze shifted to Phoebe. "Now I know why I broke my hip."

"Because you're too stubborn to listen to me even when I'm right and you know it?" Chance asked, his lips twisting into a half smile.

Phoebe leaned forward and kissed Jo on the cheek. She knew exactly what the older woman meant. There was something bigger than they could imagine going on here, the hand of God at work in someone's life.

In Chance's life.

The surgeon knocked and entered the room. After explaining the procedure to Jo and Chance, he asked the three of them to leave the room so Jo could be prepped for surgery.

"We'll be praying," Phoebe assured Jo. She wanted to give Chance and Lucy a few seconds of family privacy with their aunt so she left the room. It wasn't long before they caught up to her in the waiting room.

It wasn't easy to wait and worry. Eventually the three of them visited the hospital cafeteria for a quick bite of dinner, but then they found nothing to do other than to settle down in the waiting room. Phoebe and Chance sat quietly sipping lukewarm coffee, while Lucy flipped channels on the nearby television and played music on her MP3 player. Before long, though, the girl fell asleep, all stretched out on a small couch, her arm tucked under her head.

"Thank you," Chance murmured.

Phoebe looked up from the out-of-date women's magazine she'd been leafing through. "For what?"

Chance nudged his chin toward his sleeping daughter. "For being there for Aunt Jo and Lucy. My daughter will probably not ever admit it, but you really saved the day."

Phoebe smiled. "Lucy called 911 before I ever got there. She did exactly what she needed to do, even if she didn't think so at the time. You should be proud of her."

Chances eyes turned a glistening obsidian. "I am proud of her. I just forget to tell her sometimes, is all."

"You're a good father. Lucy is blessed." Phoebe didn't realize how much she meant the words until they'd come out of her mouth, but it was true. Chance was doing the best he could to be a good father to Lucy, and she instinctively understood that it was something Chance desperately needed to hear right now.

"I'm not so sure Lucy would agree with you on that point," he said with a wry smile. "I haven't been there for her. I don't know *how* to be there for her. Not like her mother would have been."

"You manage. Better than you think."

Chance was silent for a moment. Thoughtful.

"You have no idea what you've done today, do you?"

"Done?" she repeated, having no idea what he was

talking about. She tried to follow his train of thought but couldn't get there.

"Today. With the car."

Phoebe's heart lurched as she saw the mixture of emotions on Chance's face. She wanted to reach out to him, comfort him, but she could see the strength and determination warring for dominance with his grief, so she remained still with her hands clasped in her lap.

"You want to talk about it?" she asked softly.

Chance's gaze took on a faraway look, and Phoebe knew he was reliving the horrific car accident in his mind.

"We were on our way home from a church pot-luck," he began huskily. "It was the dead of winter in the middle of a bad snowstorm—a blizzard, really. In hindsight, we probably shouldn't have gone out that night, except that, as you know, the church is only a mile or so from the house. I thought we'd be safe enough even with the bad weather. Not that many people travel along these roads.

"I was behind the wheel." He paused and cleared his throat. "There was a drunk driver coming toward us, some guy from a neighboring county that we didn't even know. He was weaving all over the road, only I couldn't tell because of the thick fog that had set in while we were at the church."

He stopped and swallowed. Phoebe reached for his hand, caressing it gently with the pad of her thumb.

She couldn't breathe. Her throat and her eyes burned fiercely from holding back a hot stream of tears.

"I could only see a few feet in front of me, even with my high beams on. The truck was on top of me before I had time to react."

He scrubbed his free hand down his face and groaned deeply.

"I stomped on the brake and steered the car toward the curb. I didn't care about myself. I was only praying that Lindsay and Lucy wouldn't be hurt." He squeezed his eyes closed and shuddered.

Phoebe envisioned the scene in her mind and could only sympathize with how Chance must have felt in the split second that had changed his whole life.

"I didn't turn fast enough to avoid a collision. The truck clipped the back of my car. It spun out—right into a telephone pole. The whole passenger side of the car was totaled.

"They tell me Lindsay died instantly. Lucy was in the middle of the backseat and suffered only minor cuts and bruises, thank God."

"And you?" Phoebe asked, thinking she might already know the answer to her own question.

His gaze gripped hers as he reached for the black bandana he always wore around his neck. A muscle twitched in the corner of his jaw, the only hint of what this revelation was truly costing him.

Pulling in a deep breath, he tugged on the bandana, revealing a deep, ugly scar that ran from his jaw to his collarbone. "I got this."

STATUS UPDATE: PHOEBE YATES: I am in way over my head. Instead of calm and peaceful, I'm in the middle of a tempest. I'm just beginning to realize I've spent more time with pastry dough than I have with human beings. Keep praying.

Chance's breath caught and blistered his lungs as he waited for Phoebe's reaction to what he'd told her. Shown her.

He'd never felt as vulnerable in his life as he did in that one second. He had opened himself up, revealed his heart and his scars for her inspection, knowing she would now see how tarnished he really was.

She stared at him for a long moment, saying nothing. Her expression was unreadable. At least if he'd seen the shock and revulsion he'd expected, he would know what to do with it.

Suddenly her face softened and her eyes filled with tears.

"I'm so sorry," she whispered, her voice breaking.

He was prepared for her revulsion, for her to draw away from him. But he couldn't handle it if she cried for him. His heart slammed into his chest, forcing the breath right out of him.

"I don't want your pity," he said, his voice low and gruff. "And I certainly don't deserve your tears."

Phoebe straightened and looked him directly in the eye. "My heart is breaking for you, but it's not pity I'm feeling. You've come through so much, and yet you still labor to make a good life for your daughter, in spite of how you feel yourself. That takes real courage."

"Courage?" The single, strangled word came out an octave higher than his usual tone of voice. "How can you even say that?"

"Because it's true."

Chance leaned back and jammed his fingers through the curls on the back of his neck, rubbing the tight muscles there. He glanced at Lucy, thankful to find she was still asleep, her ear buds tucked in her ears and her face having lost most of the stressful expression she'd been wearing earlier.

"What's true is that I killed my wife," he hissed through his teeth.

"No, it's not. You've got to stop blaming yourself for something that was out of your control."

It wasn't the first time he'd heard this argument. Aunt Jo had confronted him numerous times about it. But it was the first time he had actually really listened.

"That's just it. It *was* in my control. I was driving. If I'd just hit the brake sooner or turned a little faster—" He let his sentence drift off into an awkward silence.

"You know what I think?" she asked thoughtfully.

He groaned. "I'm afraid to ask."

"It's just—well, have you ever considered that it might be easier for you to blame yourself and live in the past than it is to accept God's forgiveness and face the future head-on? You've trapped yourself in an early stage of grief and haven't allowed yourself to move forward with your life."

"Move on to what?" he snapped.

"To peace. To a happy life with your daughter. I know it's cliché, but I mean it with all my heart— don't you think that's what Lindsay would want for you?"

"I'd rather not think about it." She was drudging up all kinds of latent emotions he didn't want to face, never mind deal with. There was a reason he lived the way he did. Maybe not a good reason, at least not to Phoebe, but it was what it was, and he wasn't sure he could change even if he wanted to.

"That's exactly what you've been doing for far too long now. You deserve better than the paltry excuse for a life you've chosen to live. Lucy deserves better."

"Hmm," he muttered crossly. "Well, I agree with you on that last part."

"Maybe your aunt's accident was meant to be a wake-up call to you. Could it possibly be that God is trying to get your attention?"

"By hurting my aunt?" he snapped, and then immediately regretted having done so. Phoebe wasn't being cruel. She was just being—well, *Phoebe.*

"That's not what I meant, and I think you know it.

He sighed and rubbed his palms against his eyes, where a tension headache was building. He was in a tailspin, an emotional overload he just couldn't handle right now, not on top of all the other things that had happened today.

He needed time.

Space.

He was suffocating.

He opened his mouth to tell her so, but she beat him to the punch.

"I'm so sorry," she said hastily, clapping a hand over her lips. "Me and my big mouth. This is the absolute worst moment in the world for me to be voicing my opinion and giving you a veritable lecture, when here you are worried about how your aunt is doing in surgery. I can't believe how insensitive I've been."

She slid closer to him, appealing to him with a self-deprecating grin and those amazing hazel eyes of hers—eyes full of tears. Again. The woman cried about everything.

"Forgive me?"

Chance hooked his arm around her shoulders and pulled her tight against his chest.

"It's okay, honey," he murmured, smoothing down

her hair. Somehow the tables had been turned. She'd offered him her support when he needed it most. Now it was his turn to do the same for her, and in the oddest way, comforting her comforted him as well.

And it *was* okay that she'd spoken to him as she had. It might have hurt a little, but her words had chipped into the frozen glacier that was his heart in a way he hadn't experienced before.

Granted, she'd used an ice pick, but he doubted she would have been able to get through to him any other way. No one else around him seemed to have been able to pierce the armor he'd built around himself. Not even the family he loved.

"The stress has taken a toll on all of us, I think," he added, gesturing toward Lucy. "I want to thank you again for being there for her, and for Aunt Jo. I know how much they must both appreciate what you did today."

"I was glad to be there. I care for them, you know."

"I know." He swallowed hard.

Phoebe pulled her legs up and wrapped her arms around her knees, but continued to huddle in Chance's embrace. He didn't mind. Her soft, sweet vanilla scent had a calming effect on him right now.

They sat in a surprisingly comfortable silence until Aunt Jo's surgeon emerged from a set of double doors. Both Chance and Phoebe sprang to their feet at once.

"How is she?" Chance asked hoarsely, stalking

forward. He let out the breath he was holding when the surgeon smiled.

"Jo's surgery was successful and she's resting comfortably in the recovery room. I'll send a nurse out to let you know when she gets transferred back to her room and is up for visitors," the doctor advised.

"Thank You, God!" she exclaimed ecstatically. As soon as the man walked away, Phoebe whooped happily and unexpectedly launched herself into Chance's arms. Not that he minded.

"Yeah," Chance agreed with a shaky chuckle. He hugged her back, awash in relief and sharing the same rush of joy Phoebe was obviously experiencing.

Her arms were clamped around his waist and her shoulders shook with emotion. He leaned back so he could see her expression.

She was crying. Again.

"Hey there, honey, it's good news," he crooned, framing her face with his hands and brushing the wetness from her cheeks with the pads of his thumbs.

"I know," she said with a wobbly smile.

Her tears unnerved him. He didn't know why she was crying. Everything was well in the world. But even if he didn't understand it, he still very much wanted to comfort her and ease whatever turmoil she was feeling. If he knew how.

Which he didn't.

He pulled her close again, resting his chin on the top of her head, lending her his strength. She'd been through a lot today, enough to make even a resilient person like Phoebe waver and shake.

"You know, I think that even if God wasn't trying to get *my* attention today, He sure was trying to get to Aunt Jo. That woman is as stubborn as the day is long. She would never have gotten surgery on her own."

Phoebe's breath hitched, and then she chuckled. "I think you're right about that."

Chance grinned, but he didn't let her go. Not before he had to, anyway. Ultimately, Phoebe was the one who stepped away from him.

"Do you think we should wake Lucy and tell her the news?" she asked, brushing stray tears from her cheeks with the back of her hand. The girl hadn't stirred despite the clamor around her.

His gaze traveled to his daughter, who was still lying motionless across the small couch. "No. Let's just let her sleep until we're able to visit Aunt Jo."

Phoebe nodded in agreement and they both resumed their seats. Phoebe became engrossed in the program on television, or at least she pretended that she was, maybe to have the opportunity to pull her emotions together. Chance could give her that, at least, so he remained silent.

His attention, however, was not so easily drawn to the crime drama on TV. He kept glancing at Phoebe—surreptitiously, he hoped. Once he even reached for her, fingering a stray lock of her silky chestnut hair before he brushed it back behind the delicate curl of her ear. If she noticed, she didn't acknowledge it, which was probably just as well.

She was a remarkable woman, and he could no longer deny that, for whatever reason, he was drawn to her in a way he'd never been to anyone else—not even Lindsay, who had been his high school sweetheart.

This connection was different, though he couldn't have explained why. He just knew it was.

He couldn't fathom how she'd landed, of all places, in his little country kitchen in tiny Serendipity, Texas. She was a phenomenal cook, and an extraordinary person altogether. What was she doing here?

He didn't know. But thank God that she'd come into his life when she did. He had no idea how this day might have played out had she not been there. Lucy most certainly would have been worse for the wear.

Thank God, he thought again, and then he paused. Was that really what he meant, or was it just cliché to think that way? Phoebe had accused him of holding on to his anger at himself to keep from his having to face the future, and maybe she was right.

He was angry with himself. But he'd been angry with God, too, he now realized. The question had always haunted him: Why had God taken Lindsay away from him?

The answer wasn't simple. Maybe there was no

answer for him, at least not in this lifetime. But he'd been raised to believe God was merciful, and that all things worked together for good for those who loved Jesus Christ.

God hadn't changed. He hadn't moved. He hadn't disappeared the night Lindsay had died.

Chance had done all of those things. So maybe God had been there all along, even when Chance had been too blinded with grief to see it.

What had Phoebe said back when they were arguing on the road earlier?

God forgives you.

It troubled him to admit it, but maybe it *was* his own pride standing in the way of his once vibrant relationship with God.

His arrogance, his lack of faith, had damaged more than just himself. He was hurting Lucy and Aunt Jo. And it had taken a caring, sometimes brutally candid woman to make him see the light.

He wished he would have had time to pray about it, but at that moment, a nurse arrived and indicated that Aunt Jo was back in her room and up to seeing visitors.

"Hey, Luc," he said, gently shaking his daughter's shoulder. "Wake up. We can go see Auntie Jo now."

Lucy popped up to a sitting position, her eyes wide. "Is she okay? Did the surgery work?"

"She's fine, honey," Phoebe assured her, moving

to Chance's side. "Like your father said, she's ready for visitors, so you can see for yourself."

Lucy beamed and Chance's breath hitched. His little girl—teenager, whatever—meant all the world to him. Most of the time he didn't even feel like they were speaking the same language, but he loved her just the same. He thought he ought to tell her so.

As for Phoebe—well, he'd have to sort through his feelings for her later.

As soon as they'd entered Aunt Jo's room, he moved to her side and brushed her salon-curled red hair off of her forehead with his palm.

"How are you feeling?" He asked the question that was at the forefront of everyone's minds.

Jo scowled, although her outward annoyance didn't reach her eyes. "How do you think I'm feeling? Like someone just jammed a hot metal poker into my side, if you must know."

Everyone chuckled in relief. Aunt Jo hadn't lost any of her sass just because of some old operation.

"And did you know they mean to keep me in here nearly a week to recover? A *week!* How am I supposed to keep the café running from a hospital bed?"

"Don't you worry about the café," Phoebe admonished. "Chance and I will be able to handle it just fine on our own. The only thing we want you thinking about right now is getting well."

"I hate to be a burden on y'all," Jo said with a dramatic sigh.

"Apparently you weren't listening earlier," Chance admonished her. "You are not, nor will you ever be, a burden to us."

Aunt Jo smiled weakly. She would never say so, but Chance could tell the surgery had taken its toll on her.

"We should go and let you sleep," Phoebe murmured, apparently having come to the same conclusion.

"I'm not the only one who needs to be sleeping. I want you guys to get out of here and get some shut-eye as well. And I will not have you arguing with me on this one. I'm just going to be groggy right now, anyway."

Chance chuckled and nodded, although the thought of getting back into a car again didn't thrill him. But now that he'd taken the first step, he knew it was imperative that he continue down the road to recovery. He needed to keep getting back up on that horse until he was no longer afraid of it.

Besides, he had no other way to get home.

"We'll be back first thing in the morning," he assured her.

"But the café—"

"Will be closed. At least for tomorrow." He gestured for Phoebe and Lucy to exit. They each kissed Aunt Jo on the cheek before leaving.

"You really don't have to—"

"Not listening," Chance informed her in a singsong

voice. He leaned over and kissed his aunt on the forehead. "Now get some sleep."

Chance was out the door before his aunt could argue any further. Phoebe and Lucy met him in the hallway.

"Why don't you girls head on out to the car?" he suggested. "I have one more quick stop to make."

Phoebe questioned him with her eyes. He smiled but did not answer her unspoken question.

"I'll be right behind you," he assured them.

There was just this one thing. It wouldn't take long, and he needed to do it alone.

Find the chapel.

He had a life to rededicate to the Lord.

Chapter Eleven

STATUS UPDATE: PHOEBE YATES: Thank you all for your prayers. My friend's surgery was successful and she's recovering nicely. Now if we can just get her to rest until her wounds are healed...

JOSEPHINE HAWKINS MURPHY: You can use the internet from your cell phone while recuperating in the hospital. Who knew?

Over the course of the next week, Phoebe and Chance tag-teamed cooking the meals at the café and visiting with Jo. Even the hospital staff had a hard time keeping her down—not when she wanted to be up and about.

Once Chance had gotten over his initial reluctance to ride in a car, it hadn't taken much to get him back behind the wheel, and so he was able to make the daily trip to the hospital on his own. Phoebe was thankful for that blessing.

In many ways he was like a new man. Much of his gruffness and surly attitude was gone—he'd even attended church with everyone on Sunday. Emerging was the kind, gentle-hearted man Phoebe had known he'd always held inside.

Amazing what a good boost to a man's self-confidence conquering his own fears could be. Or at least, Phoebe thought that must be what she was witnessing, because she couldn't think of any other reason for the change. In any case, she was glad for him and for his family.

Now that Aunt Jo, as Phoebe was unconsciously beginning to think of her, was home from the hospital and they didn't have the two-hour roundtrip drive, running the café wasn't quite so difficult. She and Chance still didn't see much of each other, though, as someone always had to be at home to make sure Aunt Jo followed the *bed* part of bed rest and to have someone by her side when she took in her daily recuperative exercise.

The situation continued to be taxing on Phoebe both mentally and physically, and she found she was beginning to feel the effects of long hours and little sleep.

After a long, busy Friday at the café, she was looking forward to nothing more than putting her feet up and watching some television at home with Lucy—er, at the Hawkinses' home, rather.

But the moment she walked into the house, she knew something was wrong. The television wasn't blaring, for one thing. Lucy always had the TV on, whether or not she was watching it. It was the silence that unnerved Phoebe.

Aunt Jo was, hopefully, in her room resting; but Lucy should have been home. Where was she?

Curious, Phoebe decided to track down Lucy and see what was going on. It didn't take her long. She found the girl huddled up on the oversized easy chair in the family room. Lucy was staring off into space, and Phoebe could tell she'd been crying. Most tellingly, there was no sign of the girl's cell phone or MP3 player, the two devices Lucy was never without. Chance had often teased that they were extensions of Lucy's hands, which usually resulted in the girl rolling her eyes.

Phoebe took a seat on the couch opposite her.

"What's up, hon?" she asked gently. She tried to catch Lucy's gaze but the girl looked away from her.

"Nothing," Lucy muttered.

"Really? Because if I had to guess, I would say this is about a boy." It was a shot in the dark, a random guess, meant to make Lucy laugh.

Instead, she burst into tears.

So it *was* about a boy. Phoebe's track record with men was less than stellar, but she supposed she ought to be able to share some junior-high-aged wisdom with the girl.

"Brian?" she prompted gently when Lucy didn't offer anything.

Lucy sniffled and shook her head. "Michael Avery."

Phoebe quickly wrapped her mind around this new piece of information. Teenage girls were especially flighty when it came to their love lives, so she wasn't really surprised that Lucy had moved on to new territory, just caught off guard a little bit.

"You want to tell me about him?"

Lucy's eyes brightened through her tears and she sighed dramatically. "He's so chill."

"Chill?" Phoebe obviously wasn't in touch with the current teenaged lingo. "Does that mean he's cute?"

"Super cute." Lucy flashed her a wavering smile.

"And he goes to your school?"

"He'll be in ninth grade next year and will go to the high school. Don't tell Dad, though. He'd pitch a fit."

Phoebe chuckled.

"It's our secret, then," she said, making a zipping motion over her lips and crossing her heart. "So what's the deal with this guy?"

Lucy studied her for a moment as if deciding what and how much she wanted to reveal. Phoebe wasn't offended. They'd been through a lot in the past couple of weeks, but she was still a relative stranger to Lucy. Still, it was clear the girl needed to talk to somebody. She gave her an encouraging smile and waited.

Finally, Lucy sighed. "The Sadie Hawkins dance is coming up."

"But you're out of school for the summer," Phoebe commented, confused.

"Yeah. It's something the community puts on for the kids in town in the summer, I guess to keep us out of trouble or something."

"Sadie Hawkins. Is that the one where the girl asks the guy?"

Lucy nodded glumly.

"And this Michael turned you down?"

Poor Lucy. She'd had a rough couple of weeks as it was. She really didn't need a rejection from the guy she had a crush on to add to the list.

"Uh-uh." Lucy shook her head. "I haven't asked him."

"Because…?"

"I don't want him to say no."

"So instead, what? You're not going to go at all? You know it's perfectly fine for a girl to ask a guy out in this day and age, especially for Sadie Hawkins, where it's expected. You may as well take advantage of it."

"Maybe I'll just go with some of my friends," she said miserably.

"You could do that," Phoebe agreed, leaning forward. "Or, you could use that as a back-up plan. First you ask Michael to the dance, and if he doesn't want to go with you, you go with your friends."

Lucy snorted. "You make it sound easy."

Phoebe chuckled and shook her head. "Oh, no. It's anything but easy. It takes a lot of courage to face a situation where you might be rejected. Trust me. I've had my fair share of rejections."

"Really?" Lucy sounded genuinely surprised. "You?"

Phoebe laughed. "Yes, me."

"But you're so pretty."

That had Phoebe blushing. "Well, thank you. But you know, you're pretty, too. Beautiful, actually."

Lucy frowned and looked at the floor. "No, I'm not. Dad calls me his little tomboy. Guys like girls who wear dresses and makeup."

"First of all, I can state without a shadow of a doubt that your father would be the first in line to tell you what a beautiful young lady you are. You're cute no matter what you're wearing, and you definitely don't need makeup to highlight your nice facial features. But if you want a dress for the dance, we can do a dress. Maybe even some lip gloss, huh?"

This Phoebe could handle. It would be a great deal of fun to take Lucy shopping for something other than the denim overalls she always wore.

"Even if I did ask Michael and he said yes, Dad would never let me go to the dance," Lucy said morosely.

"I'll make you a deal," Phoebe said. "You ask Michael to go to the dance with you, and I'll take care of your father. What do you say?"

Lucy brushed away her tears with her fingertips and nodded. "Okay."

"Great," she replied enthusiastically. "I can't wait to take you shopping. You're going to knock the socks off this Michael guy."

"Do you really think so?"

"I know so."

"But I still have to ask him. He might say no."

Phoebe gave Lucy an impromptu hug, and to her surprise, the girl hugged her back.

"Just remember, hon, you are a Hawkins. Your family is made from sturdy stuff. And hey—you know what?"

Lucy shook her head but looked hopeful, an enormous change from her earlier glum countenance.

Phoebe smiled and winked. "You might just be a relative of old Sadie Hawkins. You never know. If she could do it, I know you can. I have a good feeling about this."

Sending Lucy off with a smile, she prayed she was right about Michael. And about Chance, for that matter. Only time would tell.

STATUS UPDATE: PHOEBE YATES: Sadie Hawkins. That's a name I haven't heard in a while—try high school. I think I'm going to have to look her up online. If she was anything like the Hawkins family I'm staying with, she must have been one tough breed.

JOSEPHINE HAWKINS MURPHY: We are a pretty sturdy people out here in the West. Now what's this about Sadie Hawkins?

It was the end of another tiring but fulfilling day cooking at the café. Chance was cleaning the grill while Phoebe washed the last of the dishes.

It had been a week and a half since Aunt Jo had returned home from the hospital. She'd had a surprisingly quick recuperation for a woman of her age and the severity of her injuries. Not only was she up and walking, but she'd insisted on returning to work at the café, although Phoebe and Chance forced her to observe limited hours, no matter how hard she squawked that she was a prisoner in her own home. Her health came first, even if she didn't want to admit it.

As for Chance, he was feeling better than he had in years. Reconciling with God had given him not only an overwhelming sense of peace, but a new direction for his life. He was determined to move forward, not only as a child of God, but as a better father, nephew and friend.

If he could classify Phoebe as a friend. She seemed like more than that, somehow. He cast her an unobtrusive glance, knowing she couldn't see him watching her, since her back was turned to him. As always, she attacked her work with relish, humming a cheerful tune all the while.

Perhaps the most surprising part of the changes he'd experienced over the past couple of weeks was in this very kitchen. He found that he no longer resented having to share his space with Phoebe. In fact, if he were being honest, he liked having someone to talk to and share the work with. Her gleaming hazel eyes, pretty smile, generous laughter and sweet vanilla scent didn't hurt, either.

Best of all, somewhere along the way, Lucy had warmed up to Phoebe. One evening he'd even caught them with their heads together, whispering secretively to each other. They'd sprung apart guiltily when he'd walked in, which of course left him to wonder.

He couldn't imagine what was up with that, but he was grateful for the change just the same.

At that moment, as if his thoughts had summoned her, Lucy burst into the kitchen through the back door. Her eyes were wide, her face was flushed and she was breathing heavily, as if she'd run all the way from the house.

Maybe she had. Fragments of panic and alarm burst through him.

"What's wrong, Luc?" he asked hastily, wiping the grease from his hands onto the front of his apron.

As if he hadn't spoken, Lucy ignored him completely. She launched into Phoebe's arms just as she removed them from the dishwater, before she'd even had the opportunity to dry them off.

Chance's alarm subsided a little when he realized that the hiccupping sound coming from his daughter's throat was not distress, but laughter. But suspicion and a growing sense of fatherly unease edged in right over the receding panic as Phoebe began laughing with Lucy and dancing them both around in merry circles.

Something was going on here, and Chance had no idea what it was. Phoebe, on the other hand, appeared to be completely in the know.

Chance scowled. He didn't like feeling left out, particularly where his daughter was concerned— even if what he was witnessing was some kind of female camaraderie thing. His very male and very fatherly premonition was that whatever was going on here couldn't be something good.

Whatever that *something* was. He wanted to know. Now.

"Does somebody want to fill me in on whatever it is that is making you girls dance around my kitchen?" he growled, his brow furrowing.

Phoebe glanced at him, her eyes glazed over with joy, looking at him as if she'd completely forgotten he was in the room at all. She stopped swinging the

Garfield the cat–grinning Lucy around, but kept a firm arm around the girl's shoulders.

"If I were to guess," Phoebe said, her smile as big as Lucy's, "I would have to say that *somebody* is going to the Sadie Hawkins Dance."

"The Sadie what?" he demanded.

"The Sadie Hawkins Dance," Phoebe supplied. "It's the one where the girl asks the boy. Didn't they have that when you were a teenager?"

Chance's scowl deepened. "No, they did not."

Actually, he couldn't remember if such a thing existed in his time or not. He'd never been much of a dancer; and besides, he'd dated Lindsay all through his high school years. She wouldn't have had to *ask* him to go with her.

"So, your dad and I are on pins and needles here," Phoebe exclaimed, turning her attention to Lucy once again. "Give us all the juicy details. What did you say? What did he say?"

Pins and needles was one way to put what he was feeling, he supposed—sticking sharply into his skull.

"He said *yes*," Lucy cried out, her voice lined with excitement. "I can't even believe it."

"He?" Chance repeated, picking up on the only word that meant anything to him. "He, who? That Brian kid?"

He was not liking the way this conversation was headed. If Lucy thought she was going to go to some dance with some *boy* she had another thing coming.

"Dad," Lucy protested, blushing.

"Not Brian," Phoebe corrected, her smile widening. "Michael."

"Michael Avery?" Chance knew the boy. He was a good kid, but he had to be a couple of years older than Lucy, at least.

No, no, no, no, no. The word echoed in Chance's mind.

"Yes!" Lucy and Phoebe exclaimed simultaneously.

Chance had moved beyond confusion and unease into full-blown resentment. He understood what was going on now—what *had* been going on right under his nose over the past week.

All the secretive whispers. All the laughter.

Phoebe was in on this, and it infuriated him. As much as he wanted Phoebe and Lucy to get along, going behind his back and encouraging his daughter to ask some *boy* to a dance nonsense was beyond the pale.

It was wrong.

And it was totally out of the question.

He turned to Lucy. "You didn't ask me first."

He tried to keep his voice gentle, but it came out with a sharp edge just the same.

"We thought—" Phoebe started, but he cut her off with a glare.

"I don't care what you thought," he growled.

"Please, Dad. This is really important to me," Lucy interjected.

"I'm sorry, Luc. You are *not* going to this dance, and that's my final word on the subject."

"But Dad," Lucy protested, tears springing to her eyes.

"No *buts,*" he countered. "My mind is made up."

He was going to tell Lucy to go home so he could speak to Phoebe in private—ream her out, more like, as he had a lot to say to the meddlesome, interfering woman—but Lucy beat him to the punch.

"I told you," she said to Phoebe with a broken sob. "I told you he would be this way."

Then she turned on Chance.

"I hate you," she snapped viciously before charging out the back door with all the fury of a cyclone.

Chance's heart fell as he watched his daughter leave. As angry and frustrated as Lucy sometimes got with him, she'd never before said she hated him. Here he'd just rededicated his life to the Lord and had promised both God and himself that he was going to be a better father, and his relationship with Lucy had just taken a giant step in the opposite direction.

"That went well," Phoebe muttered, sounding annoyed—no doubt with him. As if she had the right.

In the skirmish with his daughter, Chance had momentarily forgotten that Phoebe was in the room—and, more to the point, that she was the direct cause of all this trouble.

"You," he roared, whirling on her in a fresh bout of temper. "What did you say to her? You two have been planning this all week, haven't you?"

Phoebe's eyes widened but she didn't back down an inch. Instead, she stiffened her spine and tipped up her chin. "As a matter of fact, yes we have."

"You had no right," he spat. "I am her father. She should have talked to me. *You* should have talked to me."

"Would it have made any difference?" she asked softly. "Would your reaction have changed if I had told you first?"

"Well, no, but—"

"This is important to Lucy, Chance. She's growing up. I know it's hard for you to do, especially given your painful circumstances, but you have to let go of her, at least a little bit. If you don't, the channel of communication between the two of you will close down completely. She's going to stop asking you about things, seeking your advice. She might even start doing things behind your back. You don't want that."

Chance swallowed hard to ease the pressure of emotion building inside him.

"She said she hates me."

Phoebe reached out to rub his shoulder and chuckled softly. "She doesn't mean it. All teenage girls are drama queens, so you'll have to get used to it for a while."

Chance groaned. Somehow this conversation had turned back on him.

"It's not as bad as all that," she assured him. "Although I have to admit that in moments like these it might appear to be so."

"You should have spoken to me, even if Lucy didn't," he insisted.

Phoebe nodded. "I had every intention of telling you, but I was waiting to see how things panned out with Michael. I saw no reason to burden you with this if it wasn't going to work out.

"I thought she'd come to me first with the news so I could pave the way before she made her big announcement. I guess she was just too excited to wait to tell you."

Chance groaned again and swiped a hand down his face. "And I just ruined it for her."

Phoebe's silence spoke volumes.

"Maybe not," she said after a long pause. "Do you have any objection to Michael Avery, other than that he wants to spend time with your daughter?"

He shook his head. "No, not really. He's a good kid. I went to school with his parents."

"You went to school with everybody," Phoebe commented wryly. "I still can't get used to some of these small-town dynamics."

"So you think I should let her go." It wasn't a question, exactly, but she answered it anyway.

"Yes, I do. It means a lot to her to know that you

trust her. You can still give her some boundaries—like where exactly she is and isn't allowed to go, and what time she should be home. That sort of thing. She gets to go to the dance, and you get to strengthen your relationship with your daughter. Everybody wins."

He stared at her for a long moment, soaking in her suggestions. It wasn't easy for him to let go.

Phoebe held his gaze. "Sorry. I'm chattering on like I'm some kind of expert in parenting. Obviously, I'm not. I have no experience whatsoever in that department."

"Don't apologize," he said gruffly. "I needed to hear what you've been saying, even if I'm not liking it overmuch."

"I don't want it to seem like I'm taking sides. Well, yes, I guess I am. But at the end of the day, you're her father. You have to go with your gut."

"Hmm," he said thoughtfully. She'd changed tactics, but he still had the feeling she was leaning on him, trying to get him to concede to Lucy's wishes. Her next words affirmed his suspicions.

"You know, easing up on Lucy and giving her a little room to be her own person doesn't mean you're not being a good father. Quite the opposite, in fact."

"Is that right?" he drawled.

Phoebe was pushing his buttons, breaking him down, and he had the feeling she knew exactly what she was doing.

"You know it is."

Wasn't that what he wanted, to be a good father for Lucy? But it was so hard to let her go, even just a little bit. Lucy was all he had left.

"I guess," he mumbled, shifting his gaze to the floor.

"Does that mean Lucy can go to the dance?" Phoebe's voice had brightened instantly, as had her expression. As if he'd be able to resist those hazel eyes. She had no idea just how much influence she really held over him. And it was probably a good thing, too.

Chance sighed and adjusted his bandana around his neck. "Yes, I suppose that's what I'm saying. She can go. But if she breaks any of my rules..."

"She won't." Phoebe cheered and launched herself into Chance's arms, hugging him tight. "Lucy is going to be so happy."

"Yeah," Chance agreed with half a grin, amused at her reaction and more than happy to be holding her in his arms. "Why don't you go ahead and tell her she can go to the dance."

"No," Phoebe said, pulling back from him and brushing a palm down his unshaven cheek. "This particular news needs to come directly from *your* mouth."

Before he thought better of it, he threaded his fingers through Phoebe's soft hair and pulled her back to him, gently kissing her forehead before wrapping his free arm around her waist.

"What was that for?" she asked, though she didn't pull away.

He buried his nose in her hair and inhaled deeply, her vanilla scent making his pulse race.

"For being my anchor," he whispered, "in a dark and stormy world."

Chapter Twelve

STATUS UPDATE: PHOEBE YATES: There is nothing more heartwarming and attractive than seeing a man with his daughter. It just melts my heart.

JOSEPHINE HAWKINS MURPHY: A man, or this man? LOL

The Friday night of the Sadie Hawkins Dance arrived before Phoebe knew it. Her time here in Serendipity was flying by at an alarming rate. She didn't even want to think about leaving, so she immersed herself in the present.

Much as she would like to have seen it, Phoebe hadn't been there when Chance gave Lucy the good news. She'd wanted it to be a special father-daughter moment, and from what she'd heard from Lucy, it had gone even better than Phoebe had prayed for.

Not only had Chance given Lucy permission to attend the dance with Michael, but he'd—reluctantly—given Lucy a clothing allowance so she could buy something new to wear for the big date.

Phoebe had driven Lucy into San Antonio that Sunday after church and they'd spent a happy afternoon getting lunch and shopping for a new dress. Now that Lucy had accepted Phoebe's presence in her life—and Chance's life—without resentment, she'd morphed into the bubbly, giggling teenager Phoebe had always known was somewhere deep inside her.

She was thankful to be able to do something special for Lucy, and not just to ingratiate herself with the girl, either. She was genuinely starting to care for Lucy—maybe a little bit more than she should. She had to keep reminding herself that soon she'd be flying back to the East Coast and Serendipity would be nothing more than a happy memory. Going to work at Monahan's in New York had once been her dream.

Now she knew she would be leaving her heart behind in this small Texas town.

"Shall we do your hair, or did you want to get dressed first?" Phoebe asked the beaming, blushing Lucy. They'd decided to use Phoebe's room for preparation, and she'd locked the door just to be on the safe side.

When Chance next saw his daughter, Phoebe wanted him to be blown right out of the water. She thought Lucy might be almost as excited about pleasing her father as she was in going to the dance with Michael. Phoebe planned to stun both guys—and Lucy too, for that matter.

"What do you think I should do?" Lucy asked.

Phoebe smiled. "Go ahead and get dressed first. That way we won't mess up your hair."

Though Phoebe didn't have any personal experience besides her own youth to draw from, she imagined the majority of teenage girls would take forever to get their clothes ready to go for a big dance; however, it didn't take Lucy nearly that long to dress.

The time Lucy saved in dressing, Phoebe used to curl the girl's soft brown hair into large ringlets and arrange it into an up-do that completely transformed Lucy from a tangle-haired tomboy into a classy, rosy-cheeked young lady. She turned Lucy away from the mirror as she worked, wanting to surprise her with the end result.

They both jumped as Chance rapped on the door.

"Aren't you ladies done yet?" he called gruffly, though he sounded more amused than annoyed. "What are you guys doing? You've been in there almost an hour already."

"And we'll take another hour if we want to," Phoebe informed him from behind the closed—and locked—door. "Now, go away."

Lucy smothered a laugh.

Chance growled playfully in protest.

"Trust me, it will be worth the wait. Now go find something else to do besides bother us, or we'll never get done."

Phoebe waited until she heard Chance's footsteps receding down the hallway, and then turned back to Lucy.

"Men," she said with a shake of her head. "They just don't understand us ladies at all, do they?"

Lucy's eyes widened and she shook her head. Phoebe could tell she was pleased to be categorized as a lady and not a child. She silently thanked God once again for this opportunity to share in this female camaraderie with Lucy, and humbly recognized that it was something she was in a unique position to do.

Aunt Jo, for all her quirks, was a die-hard T-shirt and jeans woman. Shopping for dresses, much less preparing for fancy dates, was simply not in her nature. The older woman understood the importance of what was happening, though, and joyfully stepped aside so Phoebe and Lucy could bond. She was, Phoebe presumed, waiting in the living room with almost as much anticipation as Chance was, though with a great deal more understanding of the female mind at work.

If it had only been Chance here to navigate Lucy into the heavy waters of her teenage years—well, that was too much to think about. Probably, Lucy wouldn't be going to the dance at all, much less dressed with all the enchantment of Cinderella going to the ball.

As for Phoebe, she felt like…

A mother.

Her breath caught and held in her throat as she explored that thought. She'd been so engrossed in her career that she'd rarely thought of settling down with a husband and children, even when she'd been seriously dating Josh.

But here, with Chance and Lucy, and even the wonderful influence of Aunt Jo, she'd been given an entirely different perspective on what the word *family* really meant.

Giving, taking, fighting, loving.

And she loved it—every single part of being drawn into the Hawkinses' small-town existence.

Finished with Lucy's hair, she applied a small dab of light rose gloss on Lucy's lips to complement the rich royal blue of her dress, then stepped back to scrutinize the results.

Her breath swept in and her throat clogged with emotion. The transformation was truly complete. Lucy was a veritable princess, and she had no doubt Chance would think the same.

Phoebe glanced at her watch. The time had come. In fact, they'd finished with no time to spare. Michael was due to arrive at the house any moment now, and it was important—crucial—to both Phoebe and Lucy that Chance be the first to see his beautiful daughter and have the time he needed to fuss over her before her date arrived.

Assuming Chance had the good sense to *make* a fuss—ideally without prompting from Phoebe or Aunt Jo. Chance tended not to show his emotions under that stern exterior of his. Phoebe hoped that tonight would be the exception to the rule.

"Okay," Phoebe said, smiling at the radiant young woman. "You're all set. Are you ready to see the finished product?"

Lucy's gaze widened in distress, and Phoebe chuckled. "Trust me, you'll want to see this one."

Taking Lucy by the shoulders, she led her to the door of the closet. Inside was a full-length mirror, perfect for what Phoebe had in mind. She wanted Lucy to see the whole picture, all at once.

"Okay, here we go." Phoebe turned the door knob and opened the closet door, exposing Lucy to her own reflection.

If Lucy's eyes had been wide before, it was nothing compared to what happened when she saw herself in the mirror. She gasped and brushed a hand down her cheek.

"Is this really me?" she whispered in awe.

Pride and joy welled up within Phoebe.

And love. Tears sprang to her eyes.

"You look beautiful," she said, her voice husky. "Are you ready to show your father how well his tomboy daughter cleans up?"

The tinkling of Lucy's nervous laughter sent a whole new wave of emotion through Phoebe. She mattered here. Not like it was in front of the spotlights, where no one really knew who she was, but with a family whom she cared about and who knew her and truly cared about her.

"You stay here until I announce you," she said with a sniffle and a wavering smile.

Unlocking the door, she tiptoed down the hallway and peeked into the family room. Aunt Jo was sitting in the easy chair with her knitting. Chance was pacing back and forth across the carpet, his hands clasped behind him and a harried look on his face.

Phoebe cleared her throat, chuckling when Chance jerked back in surprise. Aunt Jo joined in, all smiles and anticipation.

"She went into the bedroom a hay-pitching, horse-riding tomboy," Phoebe announced theatrically. "And now, I present to you the delightful, the delectable Miss Lucy Hawkins!"

She turned and made a grand gesture with her arms, expecting Lucy to use the moment to make her big entrance.

Nothing.

"Miss Lucy Hawkins," she repeated, this time a little louder. Had Lucy not heard?

Still nothing.

"Excuse me a moment," she said as she went back down the hallway toward her bedroom. Lucy was standing frozen in the doorway, looking awkward and uncomfortable. Her hands were clenched together by her sides.

"What's wrong, hon? This is your big moment."

"I can't go out there," Lucy whispered, her voice shaky and uneven. "Not dressed like this. My dad is going to laugh at me."

Though she knew the girl was dead serious and absolutely mortified at the prospect of having her father see her, Phoebe chuckled.

"Don't worry about your dad, Luc. He won't bite— and I can pretty much guarantee he's not going to laugh at you."

Still, Lucy hesitated.

"What he *might* do," Phoebe continued with a thoughtful frown, "is meet your date at the door with a baseball bat. That is, unless you are out there to stop him."

"Oh!" Lucy exclaimed, truly distressed. "I forgot about that."

It was enough to get her moving. She only hesitated again when they reached the end of the hallway.

"Miss Lucy Hawkins," Phoebe announced once again—only this time, she nudged Lucy into the family room.

"It's about time," Chance complained gruffly. "I was beginning to think I was going to have to—"

His statement came to an abrupt halt as he turned

and took in his first glance of his daughter in all her finery.

"Luc," he said in a choked whisper. "Can it be? What happened to my little girl? She's all grown up."

Lucy was blushing to the roots of her hair, and Phoebe suspected she was separated by a mere thread from bolting right out of the room. Phoebe gently nudged her forward, toward Chance.

He took Lucy's hands and spent a long, poignant moment admiring her. Then he brushed the back of his fingers down her cheek.

"You," he said softly, his voice full of emotion, "look just like your mother did when she was your age. Absolutely beautiful."

"Oh, Daddy," Lucy exclaimed as she launched herself into Chance's arms.

He held her tight. His bright obsidian gaze met Phoebe's, and she could see all the emotions he couldn't otherwise express.

"Thank you," he mouthed over the top of Lucy's head.

Phoebe smiled and nodded. It had been her pleasure.

Really.

Aunt Jo clapped her hands in delight. "Glory be, child, you're just gorgeous. But then, I knew you would be."

Chance and Lucy were still hugging when the doorbell rang.

Lucy tensed.

Phoebe chuckled. "I'll get it," she informed everyone, and this time it was Lucy thanking her with her gaze. Anything to keep her father from answering was much appreciated.

As Phoebe moved to answer the door, she offered God another silent prayer. If anyone should be thankful here, it was her. The Hawkinses had given her a gift she could never repay—the gift of family.

Chance's heart was full as he watched his beautiful, blossoming daughter and the Avery boy posing for pictures in front of the fireplace. As with everything else that had transpired that day, photographing the young couple had been Phoebe's idea. She'd even bought a digital camera for the occasion.

What a day. What a *woman*. It was one more reason to thank God for bringing Phoebe into his life—and into his family's life.

How could a man feel so completely happy and so utterly sad at the same time?

Memories flooded through him—holding the newborn Lucy for the first time. Her first words. Her first steps. Her first day of school.

And now, her first date with a boy. Before he knew it, she would be all grown up—graduating from high school, moving out, getting married.

It was overwhelming just to think about.

Happy and sad.

He was so proud of the young lady Lucy had become.

"Okay, let's go out onto the porch and take a couple more pictures," Phoebe suggested brightly.

"Excellent idea," Aunt Jo agreed.

Lucy blushed, but Michael's face was even redder. At least Chance could enjoy the boy's discomfort. He remembered all too well what *that* felt like. Lindsay's father had put him through the wringer. He wouldn't be a teenaged boy again for the world.

Not that he would go easy on the lad. As Lucy's father, it was his privilege and responsibility to make sure his daughter was safe and happy.

If this boy broke her heart…

Chance followed the group out to the porch and watched as Phoebe posed the young couple on the front stairs, taking picture after picture.

Chance kept his mouth shut until Phoebe herded him into the picture.

"Let's get a couple of shots of Lucy and Dad," Phoebe insisted, waving Chance toward his daughter. "And then we'll get some of the whole family. Aunt Jo, you need to step in here, as well."

"Isn't your roll of film just about used up yet?" he asked when Phoebe showed no signs of slowing. At this rate Michael and Lucy were never going to make it to the dance.

"It's a digital camera, silly," Phoebe told him. "I can keep taking pictures until my four gigabytes of memory are used up."

He'd known that, of course. It wasn't as if he was living in the dark ages. *She* was the one who wasn't paying attention. She was obviously not taking his not-so-subtle hint.

"Michael's mom is waiting to take them to the dance," he commented wryly, and then waved to Sue Avery, who was behind the wheel of her minivan, watching all the activity going on in front of the house with a smile on her face.

Phoebe frowned and looked down at her camera. "I suppose you're right."

Chance chuckled at the grateful look Lucy flashed at him. Apparently he wasn't the only one who thought Phoebe was overkilling on the picture taking.

"Straight to the high school and back home again," Chance pronounced sternly as the young couple made their way to Michael's mother's minivan. "And home by eleven sharp. No excuses."

"Dad," Lucy moaned. "You've told us all of this already. Twice."

More than that, if anyone was counting. He'd re-iterated the rules at least three times to Lucy alone before Michael had even arrived at the house.

"I love you, Luc," he called as Michael opened the door for her. Phoebe reached for his hand and squeezed it tight.

Flashing Michael one last stern warning, Chance waved them off until he could no longer see the minivan at all.

"They're gone," Phoebe murmured, slipping her arm around his waist. "I don't think they can see you anymore."

Chance dropped his arm over Phoebe's shoulder. They stood there on the porch in comfortable silence for a moment.

"Thank you," he said, his voice soft and raspy. "For your insight, and for caring enough to say what you thought. I would have flubbed this whole thing up. It's hard having a girl. I just want to protect her from the world—from teenage boys in particular. And I know I can't do that."

"I think every good father probably goes through this," she murmured.

"Probably," he agreed. "But I shudder to imagine how this would have turned out if you hadn't been there to step in. Thank God you did."

Phoebe stared up at him, her hazel-eyed gaze so deep he felt like she was digging right into his soul. He wondered what she saw there.

"What?" he asked as his composure thinned. She could *not* expect to look at him that way and not have him react to it. His heart was thundering, and he found he wanted nothing more than to lean down and kiss that speculative look right off her beautiful face.

And he probably would have followed his instinct, too, except that he hesitated a second too long.

She arched a brow. "I've never heard you mention God before—at least not when I wasn't pressuring you to talk about your faith."

"Yeah," he agreed, swallowing hard and wishing his heart wasn't pounding deafeningly in his head, so much so that he couldn't think straight. "About that…"

His sentence dropped off as he struggled to find words to tell her how God had changed his heart.

She remained silent and reflective while he gathered his thoughts. He was glad she wasn't trying to rush him, or he'd never get through this.

But Phoebe, of all people, had the right to know. After all, she'd been the one to knock him off his stubborn high horse in the first place.

"I owe you another thank-you," he said. "Several, probably. If it wasn't for you strong-arming me, I'd still be walking the same old lonely path I have been for years."

"Sometimes I don't know when to keep my big mouth shut," she admitted, twisting her lips.

"Sometimes," he agreed with a chuckle.

"I'll admit I can be a bit cheeky," she added.

"And it's a good thing for me that you are. You made me realize I wasn't looking at the whole picture. I saw what I wanted to see, felt what I wanted to feel. But now things are different."

"Are you saying you've opened your heart to God?" she asked, her voice raw and full of wonder.

"Let's just say that He and I now have a working relationship," he said. "That is, He is faithful and I'm working on it."

Phoebe wrapped her other arm around his waist and squeezed so hard it nearly knocked the wind out of him.

"That's the best news I've heard since I arrived in Serendipity," she squealed, her voice pitched higher than usual.

"Even better than me telling Lucy she could go out on this date?"

"Even better," she assured him with a chuckle. "The very best thing you can do for Lucy is to live out your faith in God so she can see it and emulate it."

"I sure haven't been doing that very well, now have I? I'm just glad she's had Aunt Jo to guide her spiritually while I was mucking around in my own grief. I can't believe I've been so selfish."

"God's timing is always perfect," she assured him. "He reached you and blessed you when He was ready to do so."

Chance's heart welled with emotion as he stared down at the woman who'd so thoroughly turned his life inside out. From the moment she arrived, his feelings for her had grown with each passing day.

"God did bless me," Chance agreed, cradling her head against his chest and resting his chin on the top of her head. "He brought me you."

Chapter Thirteen

STATUS UPDATE: PHOEBE YATES: Praising God for touching a special heart with His love. I'm so happy for him! As for my own heart—well, no comment.

JOSEPHINE HAWKINS MURPHY: Praising God right along with you, Phoebe. Isn't He gracious? And I'm not worried about your heart at all.

Phoebe was thrilled when Chance once again joined them for church on Sunday. If Aunt Jo or Lucy saw anything odd about it, they gave no indication that it was so.

Chance had happily survived his daughter's first date. Michael had dropped Lucy off ten minutes before curfew, and had, Chance told Phoebe as he spied on the young couple through the front curtain, behaved like a perfect gentleman, walking her to the door and *not* trying to sneak in a kiss.

That poor boy was no doubt aware he had an audience—both from his mother waiting in the van and from the way Chance not-so-subtly peeked out from behind the drawn curtain—might have had something to do with such straight-laced behavior—but Phoebe didn't suggest such a thing to Chance. She merely listened to him ramble in amused silence, glad that he felt he could open up to her.

Letting Lucy go on a date—any date—was about as big a bite as Chance was able to chew at the moment. Hopefully little by little, Lucy would earn more of his trust and the freedom that went along with it.

But for now, it was enough. Everyone was happy. Even nearly a week after the big dance, Lucy was still glowing. She told everyone who would listen how wonderful Michael was, to the point where Chance would disappear from the room when he saw Lucy coming.

Fortunately, on this quiet Wednesday evening, Lucy was nowhere to be seen. Nor, for that matter, was Aunt Jo. Phoebe thought they might have gone out somewhere together, although the entire town of Serendipity closed up at dusk, so she couldn't imagine where they might be. But she'd recently seen them with their heads together, speaking in low tones about some project or other. Maybe that was it.

In any case, Phoebe was looking forward to putting her feet up and relaxing with a good book. Apparently, it wasn't meant to be.

Chance and Phoebe had barely arrived home from the café when Chance's cell phone rang. As soon as he answered, his brow knit in concern.

"Slow down, Luc," Phoebe heard Chance say. "I can't understand a word you are saying."

She moved to his side and put a reassuring hand on his elbow.

"What is it?" she asked softly, her breath catching in her throat. Tension throbbed between her shoulder blades. Something was wrong. Something involving Lucy. Phoebe was already praying.

"You stay right where you are," Chance instructed, his voice gruff and firm. "Phoebe and I will be right there."

"What is it?" she asked again as he ended the call.

"I don't know. I could barely understand her, she was talking so fast—and her voice was all high and wavery. She was talking about Aunt Jo, I think," he explained, fishing in his pocket for the keys to his SUV.

"What did she say?"

"Well, as near as I could make out, Aunt Jo needs us for something. I hope she didn't fall and hurt herself again. Lucy said to hurry."

"I'm right behind you," she assured him, swiping her purse from the counter. "Let's go."

Chance made the drive from the house to the café in record time. Phoebe thought he probably wasn't even aware he was speeding. His entire focus was on getting to Lucy and Aunt Jo as quickly as possible.

She wished she could wipe away the worry lines evident across his forehead and the pained look in his dark eyes, but she did all she could do to keep *herself* from freaking out. She tried to calm her heart and her nerves enough to pray, but both her pulse and her thoughts were racing with adrenaline and it was hard to concentrate.

Had something serious happened again?

Chance pulled the SUV right up to the front door of Cup O' Jo and shut off the ignition. He was out of the car and unlocking the door of the café before Phoebe had even unbuckled her seat belt. It didn't take her long to follow.

Together, they burst through the door, both of them scanning the area for signs of life.

"Lucy?" Chance called. "Aunt Jo?"

No answer.

They looked at each other, their concern mounting simultaneously.

"Maybe they're in the kitchen," Phoebe suggested, leading the way. But when they reached the kitchen, they found it empty and dark as well.

"Are you sure Lucy said they were at the café?" Phoebe asked tentatively.

Chance nodded, his brow low over his eyes. "That's what Lucy said. I'm sure of it."

"I don't get it," Phoebe commented. "You don't suppose—" She didn't know how to complete that sentence without sending herself—and probably Chance—into a panic, so she let her words drop away.

"The back door is unlocked," Chance noted, going through it to peer into the back alley. "Aunt Jo's truck is here, but there's no sign of either of them."

"Maybe we missed something," Phoebe suggested. "You take the kitchen and I'll go back and take another look at the dining area."

Chance nodded and flipped on the kitchen light to begin his search.

Phoebe had barely reentered the dining room with the intention of reaching the light switches when she sensed something was different. A shiver of premonition ran up her spine.

It had been completely dark in the dining room when they'd first entered. Now, there was the glowing flicker of…

Candles?

Phoebe quickly scanned the room and inhaled sharply when her gaze landed on a single, candlelit table, elegantly set for two with fine China, gleaming silverware and sparkling stemware. The table was covered in white linen and even the napkins were cloth.

One thing was for sure—these items were not the property of the country café. And something fishy was definitely going on here.

On a separate table, Phoebe found several courses of dinner set out on china platters. Everything smelled delicious, from the appetizer to the dessert.

In that instant, Phoebe knew for certain.

They'd been had.

"Chance?" she called hesitantly, her voice cracking under the strain of how to delicately bring him in on her discovery. "I think you should come look at this."

Heat streamed to her cheeks, and she was glad he wouldn't be able to clearly make out her features in the relative darkness.

"Well, I'll be," he said, punctuating his statement with a low whistle. "What do you suppose this is supposed to be?"

"Seriously?" Phoebe asked, feeling as if she were choking. "I would think that would be obvious."

"We've been set up," he said in a low, raspy voice that turned her heart over. "The mangy rascals."

"I'll say," Phoebe mumbled under her breath. Her face felt like it was on fire. She wondered how she could possibly get out of this predicament without completely losing her dignity, not to mention her heart.

If it was possible, which didn't seem likely.

If she *wanted* it to be possible.

It occurred to her only now that a private, candlelit dinner for two with Chance wasn't exactly something she might altogether avoid—were it not for the fact that it wasn't Chance's idea in the first place. Lucy and Aunt Jo had set them up—and they were probably still hanging around to see the results of their labor.

Crazy matchmakers. What had they been thinking?

While it seemed exactly the kind of thing Aunt Jo might do, Lucy's involvement didn't make sense. Setting Phoebe up with her father?

She couldn't comprehend how this major turn of events had happened, but she knew it was true just the same.

"So?" Chance asked, his breath warm on her ear.

She hadn't realized he was so close to her. Near enough for him to wrap her in his arms and...

"S-so, what?" she stammered.

"Do you want to let all this good food go to waste, or shall we accept the unspoken offer and dine together?"

There was humor lining his voice. She was sure of it.

He thought this was funny?

This situation was many things, but in Phoebe's opinion, funny wasn't one of them.

"What's so amusing?" she snipped.

He broke into a full-blown belly laugh, something

Phoebe had rarely heard from him, at least beyond his occasional wry chuckle.

She liked it.

She turned halfway, trying to read the expression on his face. Though it wasn't easy to see in the dark, it was clear the worry lines were gone, replaced by a real smile and the reflection of the flickering candle-light making the amusement glow in his eyes.

"Apparently I'm not the only one you've managed to impress since you've been here," he remarked.

"Oh," she groaned. Surely he didn't think she had tried to influence Lucy or Aunt Jo to throw the two of them together as a couple. "I didn't—"

"I'm just teasing," he cut in, his grin widening.

Obviously, Chance wanted to get the full mileage from this situation, although Phoebe wasn't sure why.

"Shall we?" he asked, moving forward and pulling out a chair for her.

"I feel like we should have dressed up," Phoebe admitted, feeling suddenly unsure of herself. "I have grease on my jeans."

Chance laughed. "Honey, you are forgetting this is Serendipity. Wearing greasy jeans *is* dressing up."

Reluctantly, she allowed him to seat her. "In that case, I accept."

"As do I," said Chance, sotto voce. He glanced around the area, presumably wondering, just as Phoebe was, where Lucy and Aunt Jo might be hiding. Clearly his loud, emphatic statement was for their benefit.

Phoebe had no doubt the two devious matchmakers *were* still around—somewhere. Probably observing the situation with glee and patting themselves on the back for their unmitigated success.

But in Phoebe's mind, the journey had only just begun. Success was a long way down the road, farther than she could see right now. Exploring, out in the open, the possibility of a relationship with Chance beyond what they shared in the kitchen was terrifying to her.

It might fail.

And she suddenly realized she cared very much about the outcome. There were so many obstacles yet in their way, including the fact that she was supposed to leave in a week, not to mention the fact that Chance was still grieving over Lindsay.

But right here, right now, with their gazes meeting over the muted, dreamy glow of the candlelight, none of that seemed to matter.

They were just a man and a woman, sharing a wonderfully romantic dinner.

Apparently Chance was having the same thought.

"So, Ms. Yates," he said, leaning forward on his elbows and flashing her a sly grin, "this wasn't exactly how I'd planned for it, but it appears we are now on our first official date."

Did that mean he'd thought about planning a date on his own? Did it even matter now?

Though it was empty, he lifted his glass and toasted her. "To a beautiful woman and a wonderful evening."

STATUS UPDATE: PHOEBE YATES: Oh, dear.

JOSEPHINE HAWKINS MURPHY: ;-)

Chance might never have gotten there on his own. Asking Phoebe on a date, that is.

It had been fifteen-plus years since he'd been on the dating scene, and at that time he'd been a cocky, arrogant teenage boy with the world at his feet. And once he'd started going out with Lindsay, he'd dropped right out of the dating pool altogether.

So to say he was rusty on his courting skills would be an understatement. A *gross* understatement.

Yet here they were, he and Phoebe, sitting across from each other enjoying a romantic dinner for two, thanks to his sneaky daughter and interfering aunt.

The both of whom, now that he thought about it, had to be lurking somewhere close, watching them. He hadn't heard Aunt Jo's truck revving up, and he knew he would have, if they had left. Aunt Jo's Ol' Bessie roared like a monster when the ignition was turned, and it was too quiet here in the café for him not to have noticed.

Which meant they were still hanging around, the little spies.

"Shall I get us something to drink from the kitchen?" he asked Phoebe, thinking that would give him the opportunity to do a little snooping of his own.

Phoebe apparently didn't realize his intentions. "We've got a carafe of tea and a bucket of ice right here."

"Oh, good," he said, settling back into his seat. He didn't know how to communicate his intentions to Phoebe, so he moved on to plan B.

He'd purposefully seated himself facing the kitchen, knowing it was unlikely that the matchmaking duo would be able to restrain themselves from glancing in to see the result of their handiwork.

He wasn't mistaken.

He and Phoebe were halfway through their salads when he spotted two scheming sets of eyes peeking out from behind the service counter. He would have laughed if it wouldn't have given him away. He wasn't sure he wanted to let Lucy and Aunt Jo know he was on to them. Not just yet.

In fact, come to think of it, he could really have some fun with this situation.

Oh, yes. Two could play at this game. Or *four*, as the case may be.

Chance dropped his fork and reached for Phoebe's hand across the table, giving her his best

totally-infatuated-with-a-beautiful-woman stare. For
Lucy and Aunt Jo's benefit, of course—although admittedly it was not a difficult role for Chance to play.

He had always been aware of Phoebe's outer
beauty—her sparkling hazel eyes and genuine smile
were hard to miss. But now that he knew her better,
he was equally—if not more—attracted to the inner
beauty of her spirit. She was strong and independent,
a woman who lived her faith every moment of every
day, a habit Chance could only aspire to.

"Don't look now," he said, his voice low enough
not to be heard across the room—or in the kitchen,
to be precise, "but we have an audience."

Phoebe tensed and the pressure of her hands in his
increased. It was hard to be sure in the muted candle-
light but he thought she might be blushing. Most certainly, she dropped her gaze to the table and wouldn't
look up. It was the first time he'd ever seen Phoebe so
disconcerted about anything, and it gave him pause
for thought.

Was it bothering her this much to be sharing an
intimate dinner with him? Or was it simply that she
was uncomfortable being watched?

There was one way to find out—by turning the
tables on their silent spectators and observing how
Phoebe reacted.

"It occurs to me that maybe we could give them
something to watch, seeing as they went to all this
effort for us. What do you say?"

Phoebe smiled and visibly relaxed, and impish gleam appearing in the hazel depths of her eyes. His breath caught. He could get lost in that gaze.

"It would serve them right," she whispered. "I'm all in. What did you have in mind?"

Chance decided to show her rather than tell her. He drew her left hand to his lips, gently kissing first the back, and then the palm. He wasn't sure if the shiver he felt came from him or from Phoebe.

"Darling," he said, his voice loud and clear. "At last, we can be alone together. I've been waiting for this moment for weeks now."

Which was not a total lie. In fact, it was the stone-cold truth, even if he hadn't realized it until he'd said the words aloud.

Phoebe snatched her hands back, clasping them in her lap. She lifted an eyebrow and leaned forward.

"That's a little bit of an overkill, don't you think?" she whispered, her face crinkling adorably.

Chance shrugged. "I'm just trying to give them their money's worth," he said, matching her low tone.

"I didn't know my feelings were so obvious," Phoebe said in a raised voice. "How do you think Lucy and Jo knew what was happening?"

Stunned at her words, Chance swallowed hard. Phoebe was playing along with the game he'd staged, but the question remained—how *had* his family figured out he was falling for Phoebe? He hadn't even really known himself until just now.

"They must have seen me mooning about like a lovesick calf," he answered.

Phoebe's wide-eyed gaze snapped to his. Now he really *had* gone over the edge. *Mooning like a lovesick calf?* Nobody actually talked that way in real life, least of all him.

"Perhaps they know us better than we know ourselves," Phoebe commented thoughtfully, reaching for a covered dish. "Green bean casserole?"

Chance nodded absently and held out his plate to her. "Maybe they do," he agreed.

And maybe they did.

It was quiet for a few minutes as Phoebe dished out the main course of honey-baked spiral ham, mashed potatoes and broccoli to go along with the green bean casserole. The food looked and smelled delicious. Aunt Jo must have slaved all day to cook such a meal.

He'd have to remember to thank her—after he'd reamed her out for being a nosy old busybody. Which, of course, she was. Oddly, though, Chance didn't seem to care. At least right now, he didn't.

He'd just taken his first bite of ham when he heard Aunt Jo's truck engine roar to life and putter off down the road.

"Finally," he said with a sigh that was half relief and half appreciation for the mouthwatering ham he'd just swallowed. "I was starting to wonder if they would ever leave."

Phoebe put a hand over her heart. "I've never been so nervous in my life."

Chance's brow rose. "Nervous because of them watching us, or nervous because you have to share this dinner with a gruff old man?"

"You're not old," Phoebe corrected absently.

Chance laughed. "No, just gruff. Is that what you are saying?"

"No," Phoebe responded, sounding appalled. "You're twisting my words. I didn't mean to imply that you're—"

"I'm just teasing," he cut in. "Besides, I'm the first to admit I haven't made it easy for you to spend time with me. I'm surprised you didn't cut and run that first day."

"I do *not* back down from challenges," she protested.

Chance laughed again. "So I've noticed."

She dropped her gaze and focused on cutting a dainty little bite of ham. Chance picked up his own fork, but he didn't immediately turn his attention to his food, as good as that was.

This date, he realized, altered the whole playing field, at least for him. Like rededicating his life to the Lord and getting behind the wheel of a car, admitting he had feelings for Phoebe was a monumental step forward, one with tremendous consequences.

He wanted to explore this relationship, now that he'd acknowledged it, but he was running out of time.

Phoebe would be leaving Serendipity in—what? One week? Two?

Was a relationship even possible?

He didn't know the answer to that question, only that he had to try to make it work.

"What?" Phoebe asked when she noticed him staring at her. "Aren't you going to eat?"

"Sure," he said, jabbing his fork into the green beans. "I was just thinking—you know my life story, but I hardly know anything about you, comparatively."

"There's not much to tell," she protested; but in the end, with Chance plying her with questions, he learned a great deal.

She was born in New York City, an only child. Her parents owned a small but exclusive restaurant where Phoebe had first acquired her love of the culinary arts. He already knew she had gone abroad at least one time during her studies, but now she regaled him with stories of the places she'd been and the people she'd met.

Before they knew it, they'd finished dinner and had enjoyed ample slices of Phoebe's own peach pie for dessert. Phoebe insisted on cleaning up before they left, although Chance privately thought Lucy and Aunt Jo should be responsible for the mess they'd created.

It wasn't until Chance and Phoebe had driven home and he'd parked the SUV in front of the house that he realized he wasn't quite ready for the evening to end. There was still so much he wanted to say, thoughts he didn't yet know how to form into words.

Phoebe was already exiting the car, so Chance rushed around to meet her. As he did, he saw the clear silhouette of a human shadow moving behind the curtain of the front room.

The irony wasn't lost on him. That was exactly where he'd stood when he'd spied on Lucy, ready to spring into action if Michael had so much as thought about crossing the lines Chance had set up in his mind.

Of course, nothing had happened.

And now Lucy was watching him—and nothing of interest was happening here, either.

Or at least, not yet, it wasn't.

It wouldn't be fair to Lucy and Aunt Jo to deprive them of a satisfying conclusion to their evening's work, now would it? He grinned mischievously.

Phoebe was walking toward the front door, with Chance a second or two behind her. One step, two, and he was close enough to touch her.

Before giving himself the opportunity to talk himself out of it, he reached for her elbow and spun her around, right into his arms.

Her hazel-eyed gaze was wide with surprise as he brought his lips down squarely over hers. Her shock lasted only a moment before she relaxed and melted into him. Tenderly, he slanted his head and deepened the kiss, his mind and heart spinning out of control.

Now *this* was a satisfying conclusion to the evening. He hoped Lucy appreciated his sacrifice.

No, he didn't. He didn't care if the entire population of Serendipity was staring out the window at them. All that mattered was the woman in his arms and in his heart.

If only it would last.

Chapter Fourteen

STATUS UPDATE: PHOEBE YATES: Everything has changed. If I thought I knew anything at all, I was wrong. I really don't know what I'm going to do. I've never been so confused in my life. Pray for me.

JOSEPHINE HAWKINS MURPHY: Don't worry, dear. God will provide the answers you seek.

Chance's kiss changed everything.

Phoebe told herself that she could handle it, that she was in complete control of the situation and her own emotions, but of course she wasn't.

God was. And she hadn't exactly been seeking His wisdom in the matter. Now she was praying extra hard for guidance but it seemed too little, too late.

It had been easier for her when she believed her

feelings were all one-sided, that ultimately they didn't amount to anything because Chance's heart was unavailable.

And then he'd kissed her and her whole world turned to chaos in an instant.

What was she supposed to do now? She couldn't just return to New York as if she'd never met Chance Hawkins and his wonderful family.

But she couldn't stay here in Serendipity.

Could she?

She *would* stay, if Chance asked her to. The epiphany was overwhelming. What would it be like to stay here and make her home in Serendipity? One thing was for certain—she'd never regret staying. Not if it meant a life with Chance.

She'd never been more confused in her life. Her heart was telling her to stay. Her head was only marginally more sensible, reminding her that she had an unprecedented career move waiting for her in New York. She'd be crazy to turn it down.

But she would. For Chance.

And yet here it was, Saturday, and she and Chance hadn't spoken of Wednesday evening at all. Not one word. She hadn't known how to broach the subject, and of course Chance didn't offer anything. She'd known he wouldn't. It wasn't his way.

She did catch him watching her from time to time. She would look up, their gazes would lock, and he'd smile at her—that rugged, masculine, and thoroughly charming grin of his that took her breath away. And he did little things, casual things, like take her hand when they were walking.

He just didn't talk about it.

Phoebe sighed and turned back to the cooler she was packing. Once again, the café was closed for the day in order for them to attend a community event. It was another wonderful opportunity for her to gain insight in to and experience in small-town living.

The annual Fourth of July picnic was evidently a big deal in Serendipity. This time it wasn't a potluck. Every family brought their own meal. According to Aunt Jo, the event was better attended even than a barn-raising. Everyone met at the town park to share in fellowship and fireworks.

The town couldn't afford a fancy fireworks show, of course—nothing remotely resembling New York City's. From what Phoebe had been told, Serendipity fireworks were more of the sparkler and fountain variety.

Though they weren't hauling as much food this time around, it was hard not to compare this day to the one not so long ago, the day of the barn-raising. She was comfortable moving about the house now, getting what she needed for the picnic. She *lived* here, in a way she'd never done in her solitary New York apartment.

An even bigger blessing was her newfound relationship with Lucy. The girl had gone from openly resenting Phoebe's presence in their family to setting her up on a date with her dad.

"You look lost in thought," Chance said, coming up behind her and wrapping one arm around her shoulders and the other around her waist. He was so close she could feel his warm breath on her neck, inhale the rugged, musky aftershave he always wore.

"Just thinking about today," she said, closing her eyes and enjoying the moment.

It was the first time Chance had held her in his arms since Wednesday night, and she was loath to pull away, but she quickly jolted forward and out of his reach when Aunt Jo bustled into the kitchen with Lucy hot on her heels.

The gleam of approval in Aunt Jo's eyes was hard to miss, and it made Phoebe uncomfortable. Matchmaking aside, expressing a romantic interest in Phoebe was a huge life change for Chance. Aunt Jo had to know it wouldn't be easy.

"Everybody ready?" the older woman asked.

"Good to go," Chance answered, reaching for the packed cooler. "Food—check. Family—check. Fireworks—check."

Phoebe hadn't seen any fireworks. Apparently Chance had taken care of that detail.

"And for Lucy," Phoebe teased, winking at the teen, "her cell phone and MP3 player."

"Although why she thinks she needs to bring her

cell phone is beyond me. Every single one of her friends will be right there with her in the park."

Lucy rolled her eyes. "Who declared this National Pick on Lucy Day? I thought it was the Fourth of July."

Everyone laughed, and Phoebe marveled at how relaxed and carefree the girl appeared to be. It was amazing how great of a difference a few weeks could make.

But then again, *her* whole life had changed in these few short weeks.

"I call shotgun," Lucy announced.

"And I'm driving," Aunt Jo said firmly.

Which left Chance and Phoebe together in the backseat of the SUV. She thought Chance might protest. His legs were longer and he was a good deal taller than the rest of them. The front seat would have been much more comfortable for him, and he may even have wanted to drive. But he just smiled and slid into the backseat.

Not only that, as soon as they were on their way, he nonchalantly reached across the seat for Phoebe's hand, threading his fingers through hers. She immediately looked over at him, wondering what he was thinking, his making what she thought was a bold move, given that they were in the car with his family; but he was looking out the window, his face expressionless, except for the way the corners of his lips turned up, just a little.

As they pulled up at the park, Phoebe could see what Aunt Jo had meant. The place was teeming with people, so much so that she wondered if some folks had come in from neighboring towns. Chance grabbed the cooler and led the way to an empty spot on the grass, where Aunt Jo and Phoebe spread out a thick red blanket and Lucy set up lawn chairs for each of them.

Immediately, several young women came to talk to Phoebe—the same ones, in fact, whom she and Chance had been bantering about at the barn-raising. The Little Chicks, as Chance had called them.

Phoebe now knew each of them by name. In fact, she realized as she looked around, she knew *most* of these people by name. She'd seen them in church or met them at Cup O' Jo. They were her neighbors.

Serendipity was so completely different than the big city. She loved this little town, with all its friendly people. She loved working at Cup O' Jo, making simple pastries she could then personally watch her neighbors enjoy. She loved the rustic little church where they still sang the old, classic hymns— like "Come Thou Fount of Every Blessing" and "Be Thou My Vision."

She loved being included in the community, in the Hawkins family.

But most of all, she loved Chance.

She glanced over at him. He'd stretched himself out on one side of the blanket, bracing himself on one elbow and munching on a chicken drumstick while he watched the festivities going on around him.

He didn't join in, exactly, though several neighbors came to speak with him. But Phoebe wasn't worried. Not anymore. That was just Chance's way—quiet, reserved, allowing people to come to him instead of actively seeking others.

And that was okay. It was one of many of the quirks she loved about him, that made him different from the other people around him.

As soon as Phoebe could tear herself away from the Little Chicks without appearing rude, she went back to join Chance. Popping the top on a soda, she sank into one of the lawn chairs Lucy had set up earlier. She and Chance were alone—well, as alone as two people could be in a crowded park. Lucy was— much to Chance's chagrin—off somewhere with Michael and Aunt Jo was off visiting with her friends.

"This is absolutely perfect," she said, gesturing toward a group of elementary-school age children playing tag across the park, weaving in and out of the spots where families had set up their picnics. "There's nothing comparable in New York."

"You don't miss the skyscrapers and the busy sidewalks?" he asked.

Phoebe shook her head. "No, not really," she confessed. "I never was one for crowds."

"I thought you would be anxious to get back," he

said, his obsidian-black gaze searching hers as their gazes locked and held.

She knew he was waiting for her to say something, but what? That she didn't want to leave Serendipity? That she loved him and wanted to stay here forever?

"The owner of Monahan's is expecting me back in New York next week."

She didn't know why she said that. It was an obligation she intended to fulfill, but she knew how it sounded—like there was no doubt in her mind that she was leaving. And she supposed that was true.

Unless he asked her to stay.

And that, she realized belatedly, was the real truth. She'd said what she said in the vain hope that he would express his love for her and ask her to stay.

Only he didn't.

His lips twisted for a moment and he sat up, adjusting the bandana around his neck before speaking.

"Yeah, I remember you saying that."

Sweeping in a breath and holding it until it burned in her lungs, she waited for more. It never came. Chance finished off his drumstick with relish and then reached for another one.

"Fireworks start at dusk," he commented, abruptly changing the subject. His face was expressionless and Phoebe couldn't discern any change in his tone of voice.

Maybe she had it all wrong. Maybe their kiss wasn't as meaningful to him as it had been to her.

After all, the date had been forced on him and he had made the best of it. But maybe that was all it was—making the best of it.

Add to that the fact that they'd both known Lucy had been stealing a look out the front window when they'd returned home that night—and probably Aunt Jo, as well.

So what was the kiss, then? A show for the sake of the Peeping Toms?

Melancholy descended over her like a big black cloud. She gulped down her soda, relishing the sting of the carbonation as she tried to force down the emotion which started in her belly and swelled up her chest and into her throat.

It didn't work. She couldn't breathe.

"I forgot something in the car," she muttered, stumbling over her words. She had to get out of here or she was going to suffocate. She stood so abruptly she almost knocked down the lawn chair she'd been sitting on.

"What did you forget?" Chance asked, rolling to his knees. "I'll get it for you."

"No, no," she responded hastily, gesturing for him to remain seated. "You stay here and enjoy your chicken. I'll only be a moment."

Which was an unfortunate truth, Phoebe thought as she walked back toward the SUV. If she had her way, she would get in the car and drive away right now. It was an immature thing to even think of doing, and impossible, at that, since her car was still parked at the Hawkinses'.

Besides, as she'd told Chance on the night of their date, she was not the type to back away from a challenge—even if the trial in question was the hardest she'd ever faced in her life.

How was she going to go on with this evening pretending nothing was bothering her, when the dull ache in her stomach and the throbbing pain in her head was a constant reminder otherwise?

It was getting dark. There was that, at least. Hopefully none of the family would be able to read her expression. Hopefully she wouldn't burst into tears.

Fortunately for her, no one locked their car doors in Serendipity or she would have had to make a big production over locating a set of keys. As it was, she simply opened the passenger door and pretended to look for something.

Heavenly Father, I know You sent me here for a reason, and I know You won't give me more than I can handle, Lord. Please, please help me to be strong in my faith and rest in Your power. This burden feels too heavy for me to carry.

Phoebe closed her eyes and inhaled deeply, a long, cleansing breath. Her prayer had been the reminder she needed to buck up, turn around and go back to face Chance and the Hawkins family.

God *had* sent her here to Serendipity for a reason—

maybe just not the reason she wanted. She would have to rely on the Lord to get her through.

STATUS UPDATE: PHOEBE YATES: God has sent me here to Serendipity for a reason. I have to believe that. But acknowledging it and living it are two different things, and I'm not so good at the second part.

JOSEPHINE HAWKINS MURPHY: And I am thanking God that He did send you to us, dear. I don't know what we'd do without you.

Phoebe took longer than Chance had expected getting whatever it was that she'd forgotten out of the car. He was about to go look for her when she suddenly reappeared.

It took him only a matter of seconds to sense that something was wrong with her. She was smiling—or at least attempting to—but it was forced and wooden. Her hazel eyes were glassy and unfocused.

"You okay?" he asked, concern making the rasp in his voice even more pronounced. He wondered if she might be ill. She certainly looked it.

He stood to his feet and reached for her elbow in order to steady her.

She brushed his hand away. "I'm fine."

Chance didn't believe her. From the way her voice

changed in pitch, he doubted whether she believed it herself.

"Here. Why don't you sit down and I'll get you some water."

Her eyes widened in surprise, but she allowed him to lower her on to one of the lawn chairs. He quickly dug in the cooler for an ice-cold bottle of water, twisted the top and handed it to her.

"Are you sure you're okay?" he asked again. He couldn't shake the niggling feeling that something was wrong with her.

"Of course," she insisted. "So when do we start the fireworks? When I was walking back, I noticed that some of the other families are already giving it a go."

"We'll start as soon as Aunt Jo and Lucy get back. I'm sure it won't be long now."

As if on cue, Lucy ran up, followed by Michael.

"Dad," she asked, out of breath, "can Michael do fireworks with us?"

His first inclination was to say no, that Michael needed to do fireworks with his own family, but then he caught the hopeful gleam in his daughter's eyes and wasn't so certain anymore. His gaze flashed to Phoebe, who silently gave him her advice—just the hint of a nod.

"I suppose it will be okay." His breath left him in a rush as Lucy launched herself into his arms. "If it's okay with Michael's family," he added.

Lucy grinned and hugged him again. "We already asked. They said it was okay with them as long as you said it was okay."

So he'd been manipulated. Go figure. He'd done the same thing to his own parents when he was a kid.

Aunt Jo sauntered up, her satisfied smile indicating she'd heard most if not all of the conversation—and that she approved. Her T-shirt of the day was Land of the Free, Home of the Awesome, and she'd threaded her already bright red hair with blue and white ribbons—in her unique, somewhat excessive Aunt Jo style.

His glance moved to Phoebe. She apparently also approved of his actions. Her true, genuine smile had returned, and Chance felt an immediate sense of relief.

Talk about killing *three* birds with one stone. He'd managed to make every female in his family happy with a single sentence. It was a novelty for him, since usually anything he said only managed to get him into hot water.

"Why doesn't everybody fill up their plates before we get started on the fireworks?" Aunt Jo suggested.

Everyone agreed, and the next few minutes were spent talking and eating and laughing. Phoebe's mood appeared to have lightened up, for which Chance was thankful. Whatever had been bothering her before didn't seem to be troubling her now.

Michael and Lucy sat on the edge of the blanket,

while the adults took the lawn chairs. Chance silently, and hopefully offhandedly, observed the young couple. Lucy was talkative and flirtatious, while Michael seemed to be carefully studying his food and not saying much.

Probably nervous, if he were to guess. In other circumstances Chance might not have interfered, but he didn't even try to mistake Phoebe's meaning when she leaned over and nudged him in the ribs.

Make the poor kid comfortable.

Chance cleared his throat. "So, Michael, what are you doing this summer while you're out of school?"

Yet another comment that earned him instant approval from the ladies. He could get used to this. And once he had Michael talking, the boy lost some of his rigidity.

Before long the food was finished and the plates and utensils put away. It was nearly dark now. Chance reached for the bag of fireworks he'd brought along.

"Do you want to start with sparklers or a fountain?" he asked, digging around in the bag to see what he had available. Celebrating the Fourth of July was as much a family tradition as it was a town ritual. For as long as he could remember, it had always been his job to pass out and light the fireworks. He pulled out a long-stem lighter he kept around just for this occasion.

"Sparklers!"

Chance laughed. Maybe not so surprisingly, it had

been Aunt Jo who'd spoken. She was almost as excited over doing fireworks as the kids were.

"You want one?" he asked Phoebe.

She shook her head. "I'll just watch, thank you."

"Suit yourself." He grinned at her. "But don't be surprised if Aunt Jo has you up and waving sparklers before the night is through."

"I've been warned," she said with a chuckle.

Chance pulled three multicolored sparklers out of the bag and lit them simultaneously. Then he stepped back to watch as Aunt Jo and the teenagers dashed around, laughing and waving their sparklers in the air. He lit three more just before the first ones petered out and handed them off to the small group.

"You're sure you don't want one?" he asked Phoebe again.

She nodded. "Quite."

When the second batch of sparklers was done, Chance set up a fountain.

Lucy yanked at his sleeve and pulled him aside.

"Michael wants to light the fountains," she whispered.

"What? No. I've always done the fireworks."

His gut twisted into a heavy knot. He knew Lucy didn't mean it that way, but he felt like she was just bumping him right out of her life. The next thing he knew, she'd be asking if Michael could carve the turkey for Thanksgiving dinner.

"I just want him to feel included," Lucy pleaded, her green eyes wide. "Please, Dad?"

No, no and no, his mind echoed, but he found himself nodding, partly because he knew refusing Lucy's simple request might put another barrier between them, and also because Phoebe, who'd clearly been eavesdropping on the whole conversation, was mouthing the words *say yes* at him.

"I guess it's all right," he conceded gruffly. "As long as Michael is extra careful with the fireworks. They aren't toys, you know."

"He'll be safe," Lucy assured him, snatching the lighter from his hand. "You'll be right there watching him."

And so he would be. His role in the family might be shifting as Lucy grew older, but that didn't mean he was fading off into the sunset, even if that's what it felt like sometimes.

He was a Hawkins. Lucy was a Hawkins. And in every way but one, so was Phoebe. But he was fooling himself if he even considered the possibility that the final line could ever be crossed.

Selfishly, he wanted her with him always. But since he'd rededicated his life to the Lord, his perspective had changed. No more simply looking out for number one to the exclusion of the rest of the world. He needed to learn to put others' needs before his own. Starting with Phoebe.

Most especially Phoebe, because he loved her. He

cringed inwardly when he remembered she'd as good as told him she was leaving.

And why wouldn't she? She had a vibrantly successful career in New York and she was no doubt anxious to get back to it. He couldn't ask her to stay in this boonie town so far from what she knew as civilization and give up the fast-paced lifestyle she was used to.

He paced around a bit. He was uncomfortable and unsettled in his thoughts, and he wasn't quite sure what to do with himself now that he was no longer needed to light the fireworks.

"Sit down, Chance, dear," Aunt Jo requested. "You're in the way."

Leave it to Aunt Jo to tell it like it was. He chuckled and slid to the ground on the blanket, stretching himself out like a large cat.

He still felt awkward. Alone.

"Phoebe," he said in a low voice meant only for her. He reached for her hand. "Come down here and sit with me. It's the best place to watch the fireworks."

Her brow rose, but she slid off her chair and onto the blanket, sitting stiff and unyielding completely across from him.

"That's not what I had in mind," he whispered when the rest of the family was busy preparing another fountain. He patted the ground next to his chest. "Come sit with me."

Gold and red sparks shot up with a zinging flare. It was enough light for Chance to see the expression on Phoebe's face. She looked like she was choking on a chicken bone.

Surely it couldn't be as bad as all that. It was a simple request and innocent enough, but Phoebe looked panicked, her gaze darting back and forth between Aunt Jo and the teenagers and then back to him again.

So that was the problem. She had an issue with public displays of affection, at least where he and his family was concerned. Maybe that was how it was where she came from, but here in Serendipity, folks acted on what they felt. And even if, in the end, it amounted to nothing, he wanted—needed—to show Phoebe how he felt.

"Come here, sweetheart," he growled, wrapping his arm around her waist, tugging her forward until her back was against the hard wall of his chest.

There, that was better. Now he could really enjoy the fireworks, privately acknowledging that the *real* fireworks were going off in his heart.

Chapter Fifteen

STATUS UPDATE: PHOEBE YATES: It's time for me to leave Serendipity now, and my heart is breaking. These six weeks have meant more to me than I could have possibly imagined when I arrived. It didn't just change my perspective—it changed my life. He changed my life. 'Nuff said.

JOSEPHINE HAWKINS MURPHY: Perhaps not enough has been said. Not at all.

Phoebe had almost finished packing. She'd laid out her clothes for the trip tomorrow and put the rest in her suitcase. Aunt Jo had insisted she leave early from the café so she could get her things together. As reluctant as she was to go, Phoebe had eventually given in. People usually did when Aunt Jo was on one of her stubborn streaks.

Walking out of Cup O' Jo was one of the hardest things Phoebe had ever done in her life. She had so many memories stored up in her heart, from the first time her gaze had met Chance's, to the indescribable satisfaction of seeing her simply baked pastries lining the once empty case, to the way most of the café's regular patrons had stopped in to say their personal goodbyes.

She was going to miss it here, more than she would ever be able to express. She would drop all the benefits of her fancy career in a heartbeat if it meant staying on at this café, with this family.

But Chance hadn't asked her to stay, and she knew now he wouldn't. She'd given him more than ample opportunity to speak his mind, if there was anything special he wanted to say to her.

She'd experienced a moment of hope when Chance had taken her into his arms right in front of his family on the Fourth of July. Surely that meant something. She hadn't been able to pay attention to the fireworks at all, not drawn as firmly into Chance's chest has she'd been. It had been all she could do just to breathe.

She still felt dizzy and light-headed every time she thought about being in his arms, even after three days. Her pulse roared to life every time Chance came into the room, which made cooking with him in that tiny kitchen a near impossibility.

Maybe it was better this way. Maybe it was right

for her to leave. If she wasn't careful, she might just find herself blurting out her feelings, putting Chance on the spot and in the extremely uncomfortable position of having to reject her.

Anyway, what would she say? *I love you and I want to stay here?* Talk about awkward. It would be better for all concerned if she just kept her mouth shut and kept her feelings to herself.

"Have you seen Lucy?" Chance asked, popping his head in the doorway.

Phoebe jumped and put a hand over her sprinting heart. She'd been so lost in thought she hadn't even heard him approach, not even with the squeaky boards that lined the hallway.

"You startled me," she exclaimed.

"Sorry." Not appearing the least bit sorry, he flashed her a catlike grin. "I was just looking for Lucy. Have you seen her?"

"No. Why?"

Chance frowned. "She's out with Michael. I told her to be home by nine."

Phoebe glanced at her watch. "It's only a quarter to nine. She still has time to make it under curfew."

His lips twisted and his brow furrowed. "Not by much. I think I'm going to wait for her in the family room. Unless you need help packing?"

"No, I'm good," she assured him. "I just need to put away my makeup and I will be done. Maybe I'll join you in the family room when I'm finished."

He gave her a strained nod. "Please do. I'm not certain I'm going to handle this well if she is late. It would probably be good for you to be there to help me temper my reaction."

Phoebe chuckled and shook her head. She felt sorry for Lucy if the poor girl broke curfew. But a few moments after Chance left, Lucy appeared in the doorway.

"Oh, good," Phoebe said, blowing out a relieved breath. "You got home in time. Your dad is about to blow apart at the seams."

"What?" Lucy asked, confused. "I've been in here since a little after eight."

"In your bedroom?"

Lucy nodded.

"Which your father forgot to check. Or else he didn't see you there."

"Apparently." Lucy's gaze fell on the open suitcase on Phoebe's bed. "You're really leaving us, aren't you?" she asked, her face falling.

Phoebe's heart clenched and she struggled to remain calm, at least on the outside.

"Yes, honey. I have to leave."

"But I don't want you to go."

Phoebe chuckled, but the sound was flat even to her own ears. "I remember a time in the not-so-distant past when you didn't want me in this house at all. Besides, I've got a new job waiting for me in New York. They're expecting me."

"Can't they get somebody else?" Lucy suggested, furrowing her brow in a way that reminded Phoebe of Chance. "Some other chef? We need you here."

Phoebe smiled softly and sat down on the edge of the bed, patting the space next to her with her palm. "Come and sit for a minute."

Lucy slid down next to her, her hands clenched on her lap and a quivering frown on her face.

"I can't stay," Phoebe explained gently. "This has been the best six weeks of my life, but all along we knew this wasn't a permanent arrangement."

"It could be," Lucy stated adamantly.

"How is that?"

"If you married my dad."

Whatever Phoebe had thought Lucy might say, this was not it. Her face flamed with embarrassment even as her heart filled with longing for what could not be.

"I can't do that," she managed to choke out.

"Why not?" Lucy asked sagely. She stood to her feet and turned to face Phoebe. "I, for one, think it's a great idea. And I know Aunt Jo will agree with me."

"Well, first of all, your father hasn't asked me. And secondly—"

"So ask him."

"I beg your pardon?" Phoebe was flabbergasted.

"Just ask him. I'll bet he'd say yes."

"I can't do that," she protested, her heart fluttering in her throat.

"Why not? You were the one who said it was perfectly fine for a girl to ask a guy out."

Phoebe cringed. She'd never expected *those* words to come back to haunt her.

"That was for the Sadie Hawkins Dance," she explained, her words pained. When she'd originally said so to Lucy, she hadn't meant Sadie Hawkins at all. It *was* perfectly fine for Lucy to ask a guy out. Phoebe just wasn't that brave. "You were supposed to be the one who asked Michael to the dance, not the other way around."

"So be like Sadie Hawkins," she implored. "You have to try. Think about it. Then you'd be Phoebe Hawkins. How chill would that be?"

"Very chill," Phoebe agreed with a sigh. "But I just can't do it. I'm sorry, Lucy."

Lucy bolted to her feet and ran from the room, tears streaming down her face. Phoebe realized her own cheeks were wet, as well. She'd never in a million years want to hurt Lucy in any way. She'd come to love the girl like the daughter she'd never had.

But she couldn't ask Chance to marry her. Sure, it was the twenty-first century, and she had no problem acknowledging that when it came to male/female relationships, as she'd told Lucy, it was perfectly okay for a woman to do the asking—even so far as proposing to their special man.

But it wasn't right for Phoebe, no matter how much Lucy pleaded with her. No matter how much she loved Chance. No matter that there would never be another man in her life who could ever take his place in her heart.

No matter how her heart was breaking.

She wouldn't do that to Chance—put him on the spot and force him to reject her personally. She was a little worried though, because she doubted Lucy had the same qualms about talking to her father, given the stubborn streak that coursed through the veins of every single member of the Hawkins' family.

It was too much to hope Lucy would let the matter rest. Phoebe had the feeling that the worst was yet to come, and there was no way to avoid it.

STATUS UPDATE: PHOEBE YATES: Have you ever wanted what you cannot have?

JOSEPHINE HAWKINS MURPHY: In the words of our Savior, you do not have, because you do not ask.

Chance was still waiting in the family room for Lucy to come in the front door when suddenly she'd slipped in through the kitchen and slumped into the easy chair, her arms wrapped tightly around herself as if for comfort and tears streaming down her face.

He'd been ready to give her a hard time about missing curfew, but clearly she'd somehow come in without his knowledge, so there was no way to confirm whether she'd been late or not.

More to the point, though, something was obviously distressing her—even he could see that, as unobservant of the female state of mind as he usually was. His protective instinct roared to life.

"What's wrong, baby? Is it Michael?" He hoped not. Relationship issues weren't his forte, not to mention the fact that his first parental response toward a boy that broke his daughter's heart would not be pretty. Still, it was a logical conclusion to guess that Michael was the problem, given that Lucy had just been out with him.

She burst into a fresh round of tears.

Feeling vulnerable himself and powerless to help his little girl, he crouched down in front of her and put his hand on her knee.

"I know I'm just your dad, and all, but you can talk to me," he suggested softly. "It may be hard for you to imagine, but I'm actually a guy, too, so I know how they think. Maybe I can help you."

She started to shake her head and then suddenly stopped, her eyes widening as she absorbed the full impact of his words. A light appeared in her luminescent, tear-filled eyes and Chance's heart clenched. He would do anything for his little girl—*young lady*, he mentally corrected himself.

"Dad, what does it feel like to be in love?"

Chance swallowed his breath and began coughing

violently. He thumped his chest hard with his fist trying to dislodge the very uncomfortable bubble of air trapped there.

Why was his thirteen-year-old asking about love?

And how was he supposed to answer her?

"I…uh…yeah," he sputtered.

He was the last person she should be going to for advice on love. He was nothing but a giant train wreck in that department.

He needed to call in reinforcements—and the sooner the better.

"Phoebe," he called loudly, his raspy voice strained. "Phoe-be-e-e!"

To her credit, she came rushing in immediately, her makeup bag still in her hand.

"What happened?" she exclaimed, dashing into the middle of the family room and looking around anxiously. "Is someone hurt?"

"Worse," he groaned. He felt like he'd been kicked in the stomach as the air he'd been choking on just a moment before now left his lungs in a whoosh.

Phoebe Yates deeply, profoundly cared about his family. Not that he hadn't already known that. He'd seen her tender heart in action any number of times in the past six weeks. The punch-in-the-gut reminder was the makeup bag in her hand.

She was really and truly leaving. He didn't know how his heart would stand it. Lord help him.

"Chance," Phoebe repeated, taking his arm to get his attention. "What's wrong?"

He glanced at her through a hazy, unfocused consciousness. He wasn't usually this emotional, but he'd opened himself up to love, and consequentially, heartbreak.

"It's Lucy," he explained through a dry throat. He gestured vaguely in his daughter's direction. "She just asked me—" he paused and shivered "—what it feels like to be in love."

Phoebe placed her hands on her hips and lifted a brow as she stared suspiciously in Lucy's direction. "Oh she did, did she? I see."

"I'm glad somebody does," Chance grumbled. "Now will you please tell her she cannot possibly be in love when she is thirteen years old?"

Phoebe sighed and shrugged. "You cannot possibly be in love when you are thirteen years old," she parroted to the girl, though Chance couldn't tell if that was for Lucy's benefit or his own. Her voice sounded odd. Strained.

"I didn't say *I* was in love," Lucy countered, rolling her eyes. "I just want to know what it feels like—" she gave a pointed pause "—to be in love."

Phoebe sat down on the couch with a thump. She raised her hands to her cheeks, which, Chance only now noted, were burning a bright red.

He didn't know what *Phoebe* had to be embarrassed about. Lucy was the one asking the awkward questions here, questions he'd thought Phoebe, given her female perspective, would be more competent to handle than he himself would be.

"So, love is…what?" Lucy prompted. "Never having to say you're sorry?"

Chance sputtered in an attempt to hold back his laughter. "Trust me on this—love is *having* to say you're sorry *all the time*."

Lucy smiled secretly. "What else?"

"It's minding your own business when someone doesn't want to talk about it," Phoebe answered caustically, although it looked like Lucy understood what Phoebe was getting at.

Chance frowned. He wasn't sure where this conversation was going, only that somewhere along the way there had been a turn in the road and he'd clearly missed it.

"Love is sharing things close to your heart," the girl countered.

"Love is knowing when to stay silent." Phoebe leaned forward in her seat, almost aggressively, her attention solely focused on Lucy.

"Love is knowing when to speak up," Lucy insisted.

This wasn't even remotely close to the conversation Chance had anticipated between the two females. It felt like a war was brewing between the two of them.

"Love is sharing your faith and bringing the other

person closer to God," Chance offered, feeling like he needed to say *something,* even if it was wrong. He thought maybe bringing God into the picture might diffuse the situation a little bit.

It sure couldn't hurt.

And it did seem to take some of the wind out of their sails. They both looked at him wide-eyed, as if they'd forgotten he was in the room at all.

Phoebe sighed. "Your father is right. Let's just get back to the Biblical version. 'Love is patient, love is kind,'" she stated, quoting the first book of Corinthians. "'It…'"

Phoebe paused and Chance jumped in. "'It is not self-seeking.'"

Lucy looked absolutely smug. "Love is finishing each other's sentences."

Chance narrowed his gaze on his daughter. "Just what, exactly, are we talking about here?"

Lucy shrugged. "Why don't you ask Phoebe?"

"Phoebe?" he repeated, looking her direction. "Why Phoebe?"

The woman had been blushing flaming red earlier in the conversation, but now she looked positively green around the gills.

"Are you okay?" he asked, concerned with the way her pupils were dilating, making her eyes appear almost as black as his. Even though she was still seated on the couch, she looked like she was weaving a little bit, so he sat down next to her and put his arm around her shoulder to steady her.

She, in turn, stood abruptly to her feet. "I have to go…finish packing," she ended lamely.

"I thought you were done," he said.

She waved the makeup bag she still had in her hand. "Not quite. I need to double-check that I have everything. I've got an early flight tomorrow."

It was a reminder Chance didn't need. He'd hoped to spend a little quality time alone with her this evening, but he got her message loud and clear.

She wanted to be left alone. She was ready and anxious to go back to her old life.

When he broke from his thoughts, he discovered Lucy was trying to sneak out of the room.

"Young lady," he said sternly. "You get back here right this minute. Park it in the chair." He pointed to the easy chair the girl had just vacated.

Her cheeks were stained pink, and she had the oddest expression on her face. He wasn't good at reading looks. What was it?

Guilt? Annoyance? Frustration? All of the above?

"You want to tell me what just went on in here?" It wasn't so much a question as it was an order, though Lucy didn't appear to immediately recognize it as such.

She slouched in the chair, wrapped her arms around a large, stuffed pillow, and stared at the ground. What she didn't do was speak.

"Lucy?" he prompted gravely.

She lifted her gaze, piercing Chance like a dagger. Tears had once again sprung to her eyes, and he felt powerless, in depths way over his head, splashing about and nearly at the point of drowning.

Even though she hadn't yet answered his question, he'd finally figured what was bothering Lucy. He just didn't know how to fix it. Not for Lucy, and not for himself.

"We have to let her go, Luc," he explained, the harshness gone from his tone.

"Do we?" Her gaze was accusing, disbelieving.

"You heard the Bible verse I quoted," he said, not liking the feeling that he needed to justify his actions. Or in his case, the lack of them. "We have to think of Phoebe first."

"Is it really Phoebe you are thinking about, or is it yourself?" she accused, her frustration bubbling over like a can of soda that had been shaken before the lid had been popped.

"Meaning?"

Lucy stood with a huff and forcefully chucked the pillow she'd been holding onto the seat she'd recently occupied.

"You think teenagers are so stupid," she accused as she rushed from the room. "But you guys don't know anything. *Anything.*"

She was out the door before Chance could ask her what her sharp, passionately spoken words meant.

He momentarily considered calling her back into the room, but at length decided to let her go. She was too angry to reason with.

Besides, she was right. He *didn't* know anything. And with every day that passed, he realized he knew even less. The big questions in his life remained unanswered.

Like how, even with God's help, he was going to live without Phoebe.

Chapter Sixteen

STATUS UPDATE: PHOEBE YATES: I'm sitting in the airport waiting for my flight. I got here insanely early. I just couldn't prolong my goodbyes. It hurt too much.

JOSEPHINE HAWKINS MURPHY: We're so sorry to see you leave, dear. You really did brighten our world—and changed our hearts.

Chance sat at the kitchen table cupping a steaming mug of coffee in his hands, watching as the vapor rose and disappeared into thin air.

Just like Phoebe.

Though he could still feel her all around him, see her in his mind's eye every time he turned around, she was gone.

Gone.

She'd left at daybreak that morning, declining the big country breakfast Aunt Jo would have made her. All the women had been crying. It was all Chance could do to remain dry-eyed himself.

Phoebe had bought each of them parting gifts— a new knitting basket and several skeins of colorful yarn for Aunt Jo, a silver locket necklace for Lucy and a bright, grass-green bandana for him. She'd said he needed to add a little color to his life.

Except she'd been the one who had brought his world into Technicolor. Now that she was gone, his life had instantly returned to shades of gray.

Add to that the fact that, if he wasn't mistaken, both Aunt Jo and Lucy were angry—with *him*.

Aunt Jo was tossing pots and pans around with so much effort, not to mention noise, that Chance was sure she was about to break something. Hopefully not over his head.

Lucy was seated at the other side of the table from him, moping and texting on her cell phone. Her MP3 player was so loud he could hear it clearly from where he sat.

It was possible he was misreading the situation. It wouldn't be the first time. Maybe they were just as upset as he was that Phoebe had left. They each had their own reasons why her departure was so difficult. But Chance had the distinct feeling it was more than that.

Finally he could stand it no longer. Setting his cup

down, he reached across the table and gently pulled the buds from Lucy's ears.

"Turn that thing off and talk to me," he insisted.

"Humph," came Aunt Jo's affronted reply from behind him. Lucy just picked up her ear buds and returned them to her ears. She didn't even bother to turn down her music.

"Oh, no, you don't." This time he took the MP3 player from her entirely and turned it off himself. "Cell phone, too, please."

He held out his hand and Lucy reluctantly complied. She'd been moping before. Now she was silently fuming. He looked over his shoulder, hoping to find that Aunt Jo had his back on this one. Instead, she was *glaring* at his back.

"What did *I* do?" he objected.

Women. Honestly.

Aunt Jo slid into the seat next to him and flopped her dish towel onto the table. "If you can't figure that out, dear, then I credited you with more brains than the Lord God must have given you."

"You're mad because I let her leave." It was a statement rather than a question.

"Ding, ding, ding. Give the boy a Kewpie doll." She was obviously being sarcastic, but at least her gaze was still filled with the love he'd come to depend on, even when he hadn't been able to voice it.

Lucy, on the other hand, was smoldering.

"Luc?" he asked gently.

"I can't believe you let her walk out of here." She looked like she wanted to add something else, but she set her jaw instead. She'd probably been about ready to call him a moron. Or worse.

And he probably deserved it.

"I had to let her go," he said defensively to no one in particular and to each of them individually, himself included.

"And why is that, dear?" Aunt Jo queried, worrying her hands through the dish towel.

"You know why," he protested. "You both know why. She has a hugely successful career back east. I couldn't ask her to give that up."

"Did you want her to leave?" Aunt Jo asked sagely, her red curls bobbing as she shook her head, answering her own question. Her T-shirt today was an appropriate I'm With Dumbo, which Chance privately thought referred to him rather than the elephant pictured on the front of the shirt.

"Of course I didn't want her to leave," he blurted out. "I'm in love with her."

Lucy snorted. "*Now* you figure it out."

"But that doesn't change anything. I'm sure she was anxious to get back to New York and her old life."

"You're *sure?*" Aunt Jo stretched out the words thoughtfully.

"Well, I mean, yes," he sputtered. "She wouldn't want to give up the big-city lifestyle she's used to and the opportunity to bake exotic pastries. She once told me she would be going back to her dream job. She'd be crazy to stay here in Serendipity and bake plain old pies and cookies at some hole-in-the-wall café for the rest of her life."

Aunt Jo's jaw dropped in astonishment. "How could you even say such a thing?" she demanded. "Cup O' Jo is *not* a hole-in-the-wall, thank you very much. It's your legacy, in case you've forgotten. Yours and Lucy's. Her middle name is Josephine for a reason."

"No offense intended," he assured her, trying to backpedal. "You know that little café is my life. But it's not Phoebe's."

"Why not?" Aunt Jo demanded, looking at him like he was a few sandwiches short of a picnic.

"Did you *ask* her?" Lucy challenged at the same time.

Talk about being ganged up on. Why didn't they just give him a break?

And then, slowly and pointedly, Lucy's words sank into his thick brain.

Had he *asked* Phoebe if she'd wanted to stay?

He had prayed about it and asked God to help see him through, but he'd made assumptions where Phoebe's wishes were concerned. He'd jumped to his own conclusions about what was best for her without even bothering to consult her first and ask her what *she* wanted.

He blanched and couldn't take a breath. He hadn't even given her a choice, offered her the option to stay if she wanted to. In fact, through his own erroneous words and actions, he'd actually pushed her away, giving her no reason to believe she was welcome here permanently.

He hadn't told her that he loved her.

What an idiot he was. No wonder Aunt Jo and Lucy were so put out with him.

He stood to his feet with such alacrity that he knocked the table with his thigh and sloshed coffee all over the surface.

"I'll get it," Aunt Jo said, mopping the liquid up with her dish towel.

"I've got to go," he announced.

"We know, dear," Aunt Jo said calmly, but both she and Lucy gave Chance a spontaneous hug.

Shot with adrenaline at this sudden decision, he was shaking from head to toe. His mind was darting a million places at once.

Focus, he told himself. He had to pull it together, and fast, if he was going to logically figure out exactly where she'd gone and, equally important, how to catch up with her before she disappeared for good.

"Do you know which airport she's heading for?" he asked as he shrugged into his trench coat and planted his cowboy hat on his head, adjusting the brim low over his brow as he always wore it. On a whim, he grabbed the green bandana and tied it around his neck, replacing the worn black one.

"I can do you one better," Aunt Jo replied, the curls in her red hair bouncing in all her excitement. "Phoebe gave me the name of the airline and the flight number before she left. Because I had the foresight to ask for it, of course."

He kissed his aunt noisily on the cheek. "You're brilliant."

"I'd like to think so," she replied, turning him around by the shoulders. "Now go get Phoebe and bring her home where she belongs."

Chance half-frantically searched in his pockets for the keys to his SUV but came up empty.

Lucy had disappeared for a moment, but now she returned, jangling the car keys in one hand. In her other she held the locket Phoebe had given her.

"Give her this," Lucy instructed him. "Tell her she has to bring it home to me."

She opened the locket and showed it to Chance. His throat burned with emotion and he swallowed hard. On one side of the locket was a picture of a smiling Phoebe. On the other side was a recent photo of Chance and Lucy.

A family.

He had no doubt Phoebe would know exactly what this meant, much better than any words he'd be able to say, if he could speak coherently at all by the time he caught up with her. He took his daughter into his arms and squeezed her until her feet no longer touched the floor.

"I'll give it to her. I promise," he said as he set her back down on her feet and kissed her forehead.

"Now, scoot!" Aunt Jo waved him off with her dish towel. "And don't forget to call us when you get settled, dear."

"I will," he assured her.

"Love you, Dad," Lucy called.

"I love you, too, baby."

"Bring her home," was the last thing he heard Lucy say before he got in the SUV and drove away.

Bring her home.

Finally, he knew what he really wanted, and, stunned out of the complacency that had become his life, he was going after it—after her—with all his heart.

His true love.

But was it too late? Would she even *want* to come home with him?

He could only pray.

STATUS UPDATE: PHOEBE YATES: The attendant just called my flight number for boarding, so I have to turn off my cell phone. I guess this is goodbye.

It was time to board the plane and fly back home to her real life, even if that life held little meaning to her anymore. Phoebe turned her cell phone off and tucked it in her purse, and then, with a deep sigh, stood to join the line for her flight.

When she'd flown out to Serendipity six weeks ago, she'd had no idea how it would change her life. How was she supposed to face the future and pretend it had any significance for her? Everything she loved was back in that little Texas town.

She settled herself in her economy seat by the window, feeling a little cramped and claustrophobic. She could have afforded first class, and in hindsight, maybe should have splurged on it, but at the time, it hadn't really seemed to matter.

She took out the magazine she'd brought with her to browse through but it held little interest for her. Her mind kept drifting back to a certain dark-eyed, moody man who would forever hold her heart. Before long the plane was cruising along at thirty thousand feet and Phoebe was staring down the Texas landscape far below, warm tears stinging in the back of her eyes.

"Excuse me, ma'am." As distracted as she'd been, Phoebe hadn't even seen the attendant hovering over her row. Since the other two passengers were male, it was clear the attendant was speaking to her.

"Yes?"

The young, blonde woman with a sharp blue uniform and her hair in a bun smiled broadly at her. "I'm afraid there's been some sort of a mix-up concerning your seat. I'm going to have to move you to another location."

"I'm sorry?" Phoebe queried perplexedly. She glanced around. There weren't any empty seats that she could see, and there weren't any passengers waiting to take over her seat. Then there was the fact that they'd already taken off. Why would she have to change seats now?

"If you'll come with me, please," the attendant instructed.

"I don't understand."

The attendant only smiled. Gathering her purse and her magazine, Phoebe pardoned herself as she slipped into the aisle and then waited for the attendant to lead the way to wherever it was she was now to be seated. Surprisingly, the attendant was walking forward down the aisle, toward the curtain behind which was the first-class seating. She reached for the attendant's shoulder.

"I paid for economy," Phoebe explained.

"Consider this a courtesy upgrade," the attendant suggested. "Don't worry, you won't be charged for it."

Phoebe still had no idea why they would choose to move *her* to first class, or what it was about her economy seat that was in question, but she followed the attendant nonetheless.

"Here we are," the attendant said, gesturing to an empty aisle seat. It was large and plush, and Phoebe had to admit it did look good to her. "Enjoy the rest of your flight."

Phoebe sighed and moved to slip into the seat. She wasn't going to enjoy this flight, not even in first class.

"Excuse me, ma'am," said a low, raspy voice from the window seat beside her. "But can you tell me where this plane is headed?"

Tears sprang forward at the sound of that beloved, familiar voice. He'd been hiding behind an opened newspaper, but now he folded it and placed it on his lap.

"What are you *doing* here?" she whispered raggedly.

"Fixing the biggest mistake of my life," Chance answered promptly. "Telling the woman I love just how much she means to me. It wasn't easy getting a seat on this flight. I had to bribe a couple of businessmen to give up their seats for me."

Phoebe sniffled. "How romantic."

He chuckled. "I'm hoping she'll think so. I'm also hoping that if I ask nice, she might consider coming back home with me."

"Back home? To Serendipity?"

"I know it's not New York," he amended. "I think you have the makings of a wonderful country-baking chef, and I know all of our friends and neighbors will be appreciative."

"Do you really?"

He reached for her hand and threaded his fingers with hers. "I do."

She turned in her seat. She needed to see his eyes when she asked this question. "What are you saying?"

"I thought I might have to spell this out for you," he answered with the lopsided grin she loved.

Phoebe's heart caught in her throat and she couldn't breathe, but with Chance there she wasn't sure she needed the air, anyway. She would have been floating at thirty thousand feet with or without the airplane.

He reached into the front pocket of his shirt and removed a locket. Phoebe immediately recognized it as the one she'd given Lucy that morning.

"Did she not like it?" Phoebe asked, wondering if another gift would have been more appropriate.

He pressed the locket into her hand. "Just open it, will you?"

Phoebe gazed at him for a moment, soaking up the unconcealed love flooding from his obsidian eyes. How could she ever have considered walking away from this man, for any reason? Her heart belonged to him and it always would.

She turned the locket over in her hand and then slowly, reverently flipped it open. When she saw the picture of herself with Chance and Lucy, she burst into a fresh round of tears.

"Luc put the pictures in there. She said you need to bring it home to her."

Phoebe wept even harder.

"Do you have to cry at everything?" he queried with a chuckle. "I'm never sure quite what to do with that."

"Does this mean what I think it means?" Phoebe was afraid to hope, but she had to ask.

Chance put his hand over hers. "What it means, Phoebe Yates, is that I'm not the only one whose life wouldn't be the same without you. You have a whole family waiting back for you in Serendipity, if you'll have us. Will you marry me?"

Phoebe was glad they were in first-class and had the added room, because nothing on earth could have stopped her from launching herself into the arms of the man she loved. She couldn't wait one more second to hold him. Kiss him. Love him.

And now she had a lifetime.

Epilogue

STATUS UPDATE: PHOEBE YATES: Thank you all so much for your wedding wishes. Chance and I were married in the most adorable little white chapel in Serendipity. It was a small family ceremony that I'll cherish forever. My new daughter, Lucy, was my maid of honor, and Chance looked so handsome in his western suit. Aunt Jo prepared the reception and the whole town showed up. It's wonderful to have such caring friends and neighbors. I know I'm going to love living here.

I'll post pictures soon. Love to all.

* * * * *

Dear Reader,

Welcome to the first book in my new series, EMAIL ORDER BRIDES, set in the small, fictional town of Serendipity, Texas. I hope you enjoyed reading Chance and Phoebe's story as much as I took pleasure in writing it.

As Chance learned in *Phoebe's Groom*, life changes can be difficult. A death of a loved one, the loss of a job, moving to an unfamiliar town— change is stressful. If we lean on God, perhaps our life changes may bring the opportunity to start over with a fresh heart and grow from our trials. I encourage you to lean on Him no matter what your life brings. He truly is our Rock.

Next I'll be tackling Zach Bowden's story. He's the EMT who rescued Aunt Jo in *Phoebe's Groom*. Look for it soon!

Nothing makes my day like hearing from my readers. You can email me at DEBWRTR@aol.com or friend me on Facebook.

Keep the Faith,

Deb Kastner

Questions for Discussion

1. Phoebe takes a break from her high-profile chef's life by baking simple country fare. Why does she not stop cooking altogether? Can you be on vacation and work at the same time?

2. The five stages of grief are: denial, anger, bargaining, depression and acceptance. Where was Chance stuck in this cycle, and why?

3. It's difficult to experience loss, whether that is loss of a loved one, a pet, a job, status or security. Have you experienced a loss recently? How are you dealing with it?

4. Chance pushed both God and his in-laws away instead of reaching for their support. Why do you think he did that?

5. Phoebe broke off her yearlong relationship because she felt she would have been certain by then whether the relationship should be permanent. How long do you think it takes to know if a man is Mr. Right rather than Mr. Right Now? Why?

6. Lucy saw Phoebe as a threat and did not immediately accept her. Why do you think that is?

7. At what point in the novel did Lucy change her tune and decide Phoebe was the right woman for her father?

8. Do you think Aunt Jo was meddlesome or supportive, or both?

9. Which character in *Phoebe's Groom* do you most relate to? Why?

10. How did the barn-raising at the Sparkses' ranch parallel what Chance was going through in his life?

11. What is the major theme of this novel? What is its takeaway value in your life?

12. Even though Chance was in love with Phoebe, he allowed her to leave. Why do you think that is? And why did he finally go after her? What changed?

13. Aunt Jo and Lucy played matchmakers. Do you think it was right for them to intrude on Chance and Phoebe's developing relationship?

14. Phoebe had never experienced life in a small town. How is Serendipity different than a big city?

15. What will you remember most from this book?

LARGER-PRINT BOOKS!

GET 2 FREE
LARGER-PRINT NOVELS
PLUS 2 FREE
MYSTERY GIFTS

Love Inspired™

Larger-print novels are now available...

Love Inspired
SUSPENSE
RIVETING INSPIRATIONAL ROMANCE

Watch for our series of edge-
of-your-seat suspense novels.
These contemporary tales
of intrigue and romance
feature Christian characters
facing challenges to their faith...
and their lives!

**AVAILABLE IN REGULAR
& LARGER-PRINT FORMATS**

For exciting stories that reflect traditional values,
visit:
www.ReaderService.com